BLACK MAPS

BLACK MAPS

David Jauss

University of Massachusetts Press • Amherst

Copyright © 1996 by
David Jauss
All rights reserved
Printed in the United States of America
LC 95-47635
ISBN 1-55849-033-7
Set in Adobe Minion by Keystone Typesetting, Inc.
Printed and bound by Thomson Shore, Inc.

Library of Congress
Cataloging-in-Publication Data
Jauss, David.
Black maps / David Jauss.
p.   cm.
ISBN 1-55849-033-7 (cloth :alk. paper)
1. Manners and customs—Fiction. I. Title.
PS3560.A8B57   1996
813'.54—dc20   95-47635
CIP

British Library Cataloguing in Publication
data are available.

For my mother and father

It takes so little, so infinitely little, for a person
to cross the border beyond which everything
loses meaning: love, convictions, faith, history.
Human life—and herein lies its secret—takes
place in the immediate proximity of that bor-
der, even in direct contact with it; it is not
miles away, but a fraction
of an inch.

MILAN KUNDERA

Three things about the border are known:
It's real, it doesn't exist, it's on all the black maps.

JAMES GALVIN

Acknowledgments

Earlier versions of these stories appeared in the following magazines: "Torque" in *Northwest Review*, "Freeze" in *New England Review*, "Beautiful Ohio" in *Prairie Schooner* (reprinted by permission of the University of Nebraska Press; copyright 1989 University of Nebraska Press), "The Bigs" in *The Iowa Review*, "Firelight" in *Short Story*, "Brutality" in *Great Stream Review*, "The Late Man" in *Descant*, "Rainier" in *StoryQuarterly*, and "Glossolalia" in *Shenandoah*.

"Freeze" also appeared in *The Pushcart Prize XIV: Best of the Small Presses, 1989–1990*, and "Glossolalia" was included in *Best American Short Stories 1991* and *The Pushcart Prize XVI: Best of the Small Presses, 1991–1992*.

I am grateful to the National Endowment for the Arts and the Arkansas Arts Council for fellowships that enabled me to write several of these stories. My thanks also to Ralph Burns, Fred Busch, Phil Dacey, John Roder, Dave Wojahn, Deb Wylder, Edith Wylder, and, especially, James Hannah and Dennis Vannatta.

Contents

Torque
1

Freeze
16

Beautiful Ohio
34

The Bigs
47

Firelight
56

Brutality
85

The Late Man
96

Rainier
109

Glossolalia
131

BLACK MAPS

Torque

THE DAY after his wife left him, taking their three-year-old son with her, Larry Watkins took out his circular saw, attached the metal-cutting blade, and carefully sawed his 1974 Cadillac Fleetwood in half. It was not an impulsive or crazy act, as his neighbors might have supposed. He had spent almost four hours the day before making the proper measurements, drawing the cutting line with a magic marker, and chaining one bumper to the garage wall and the other to the Chevy so the two halves wouldn't spring together when he cut the frame. And in a way, he had been planning this moment ever since 1985, when he came back to the U.S. after two years of guard duty and beer drinking for Uncle Sam in Germany. To celebrate their release from the service, he and his buddy Spence had rented a limousine for an hour and cruised around Virginia Beach, drinking Scotch from the limo's bar and looking at girls through the tinted glass. Spence was talking away about his plans: he was going to catch the next bus to Albany, marry his girl, and go to work in her father's office supply store. Larry hadn't given much thought to his future, so when Spence asked him what he was going to do when he got back to Minnesota, he said the first thing that came to his mind: "I'm gonna get me one of these limousines."

They had both laughed when he said that, but the more Larry thought about it, the more he liked the idea of owning a limousine. He remembered Arlen Behrens, a freckle-faced kid he'd known in high school. Arlen hadn't had a date in his life, but after he got a red Trans Am for his birthday, he started going steady with Karla Thein, one of the homecoming princesses. Larry could only imagine what the girls in Monticello would think of a limousine. He pictured himself sipping champagne in the back seat with a pretty redhead while his chauffeur drove them down Main Street. Everybody would gawk at them, even the rich kids passing in their Corvettes and Austin-Healeys, but he'd wave or smile only at those he considered his friends. If he had a limo, everyone would see that he wasn't who they'd always thought he was; they would see that he was someone else entirely, someone mysterious and admirable.

Larry knew he could never afford a limousine, of course, but he thought he might be able to build one. So after he returned to Monticello, he started collecting articles about limos and writing to *Limousine and Chauffeur* magazine for information about how they were made. He had six manila envelopes full of blueprints and suggestions by the time he met Karen at ShopKo, where she worked in ladies' apparel and he worked in electronics. She was a tall, slim blonde with green eyes and a crooked smile, and he was amazed that such a beautiful woman would go out with him. He told her about his plans to build a limousine, but she only laughed and called him a dreamer. When he picked her up for a date in his Impala, she'd say, "Oh good, we're going in the limo again tonight." And on his twenty-third birthday, she gave him a blue chauffeur's cap, climbed into the back seat, and said, "Once around the park, then home, James!" She teased him, but Larry knew she was looking forward to the day when he'd build his limousine and drive her around town like a queen.

Then, a few months after he and Karen were married, he bought the Caddy from Hawker's Salvage and had it towed to his garage. He thought Karen would be pleased, but when she came home from work and saw the rusty, battered car, she demanded he take it back.

He was so surprised he couldn't say anything for a moment. Then he said, "You can't take it back. It's not like a pair of pants that don't fit or something."

"Well, you've got to sell it to somebody else then. We can't afford a second car, especially one that won't run. What did you pay for it anyway?"

"Just five hundred dollars," he said.

"Five hundred dollars! How could you do such a thing?"

"But I told you I was going to build a limo."

She fixed him with a look he had never seen before. "Well, I didn't believe it. I thought that was just you talking."

He went over and stood beside the crumpled hood. "I know it doesn't look like much now," he said, "but wait till I fix it up. You'll have the nicest car in town. And we'll go places. We'll go all over. It'll be as comfortable as sitting in your living room, only you'll be going somewhere."

"Fix it up?" she said. "You think you can fix *that* up?"

In the weeks that followed they continued to fight about the car, but Larry would never agree to sell it. Once Karen went behind his back and put an ad in the paper, but Larry found out about it and told everyone who called that the car had already been sold. After that, Karen didn't say anything to him about the Caddy, at least not in words. If he mentioned it, she'd just shake her head and look away. Even then, he didn't give in. He wanted to prove to her that he was the kind of man who made his dreams come true, the kind of man who *deserved* a limo. But he didn't have enough money to start working on the car yet, so he just kept on collecting articles and blueprints. At least once a week he'd take out his envelopes, spread them across the kitchen table, and spend a couple of hours going through all the information.

The summer their son turned two, Larry talked Karen into taking a trip to Disney World. "Randy would love it," he said, and though Karen worried he was too young to appreciate Disney World, she finally agreed. They packed up the Chevy and left Monticello just after dawn that Saturday. It took them two long days to drive to Florida, but they managed to make the trip fun, playing License Plate Poker and I Spy and singing songs from Disney movies. But when they finally reached Orlando and Larry mentioned there was a limousine factory nearby that he wouldn't mind touring, the fun stopped. No matter how hard he tried to convince Karen that he hadn't planned the trip just to see the factory, she wouldn't believe him. While they were eating dinner at McDonald's, he asked her to listen to reason, and that made her so angry she went into the restroom and stayed there for almost half an hour. When she finally came out, her eyes were red and puffy, but there were no tears in her voice: "Take us to the airport," she said. "Now." Two hours later, she and Randy were on a flight to Minneapolis, where her parents lived. She was planning to get a lawyer and file for divorce as soon as she got there.

Larry checked into a Motel 6 near the airport and stayed up late drinking Jim Beam from a pint bottle. The more he drank, the crazier it all seemed to him: he'd actually let a car, a *junkheap*, come between him and his family. What was wrong with him? There was only one thing to do: sell the damned car and toss out his box full of blueprints and articles. And that's exactly what he'd do, the minute he got home. As soon as he made that decision, he felt as if a terrible burden had been lifted from him, and he lay back on the bed and closed his eyes.

The next morning, Larry started back to Minnesota. He hadn't intended to stop at the limousine factory, but his route took him near it and since he'd already decided to sell the Caddy, he figured it wouldn't hurt anything to take a look. Once he was there, he had such a good time watching the workmen convert ordinary Cadillacs into customized stretch limos that he decided to go through the tour again, this time taking notes. He hadn't changed his mind about selling the car; he just wanted to compare the factory's methods with those recommended by *Limousine and Chauffeur*. After he did that, he'd throw the notes out along with everything else. So he took the tour again, and when he came back out to the parking lot, he stood there for a long moment, looking at the Chevy's rusted fenders and torn vinyl seats, before he unlocked the door and got in.

Two nights later, back in Monticello, he sat down at his kitchen table and dialed the number of Karen's parents. By then, he had decided not to say anything about the Caddy unless he had to. He'd just ask Karen to come home, and if she said yes, he wouldn't even bring the car up. But if she said no, he'd promise to sell it and never mention a limo again. It was all up to her. He listened to the phone ring, then she answered, her hello cool, preoccupied. But when she heard his voice, she started to cry, and he knew he wouldn't have to sell the car. "I'll drive up to get you and Randy in the morning," he said, after she finally stopped crying.

That was over a year ago. They'd had many fights after that, and every one ended with her crying and forgiving him. But after a while—he didn't know exactly when or why—they stopped fighting. They spoke politely to each other and never even mentioned the limo, yet somehow Larry felt worse, as if they were arguing in a deeper, more dangerous way than before. And then, yesterday morning, Karen looked at him across the breakfast table and said she was leaving, and he knew this time she would not come back.

Now Larry stood in his garage, sweating in the intense July heat, the saw whining in his hand, and looked at the two halves of his Cadillac. He had been preparing for this moment for six years, and for the life of him he couldn't remember what he was supposed to do next.

The next day, when Larry didn't report for work, his boss called him and asked if he was sick. Larry told him about Karen, and he said Larry should feel free to take the day off. Mondays were always slow, and they could get by short-handed for a day. But they'd need him back tomorrow. Larry said no problem, he'd be there. But he didn't report to work the rest of the week, and though the phone rang every morning shortly after the store opened, he did not answer it. The next Monday, he received a registered letter notifying him that he'd been terminated. He sat at the kitchen table strewn with breakfast, lunch, and dinner dishes and looked at that word: *terminated*. It had a finality that he liked. He said it aloud and listened to it in the quiet house.

Although he had only a few hundred dollars in savings, Larry was glad he'd been fired. Now he would finally have the time he needed to work on the limousine. But it was too hot to work outside just then, so he spent the next few days sitting in front of a fan, watching TV. He watched everything, but he liked the nature shows on the Discovery Channel best, especially the ones about survival in the wild. Though these shows were full of conflict and danger, there was something peaceful, elemental, about the simplicity of the animals' concerns—food, shelter, a quiet moment in which to lick their wounds—that comforted Larry. Sometimes he'd tape a show and watch it several times.

Larry didn't do any work on the Cadillac, but almost every day he went out to the garage to look at it and plan his course of action. One morning, about two weeks after Karen and Randy had left him, he was surprised to find someone sitting in the back of the severed car. It was Elizabeth, the retarded woman who lived across the street with her elderly mother. She was a big, heavy-breasted woman with red bristly hair and splayed feet, and she was always talking to herself. The words didn't make any sense. They sounded foreign, even alien, and Larry always wondered if her mother could understand her. He remembered how Karen had been able to understand Randy's babble when he was a baby. He had been jealous of that ability; it had made him feel like an outsider in his own family.

Larry leaned over and looked in at Elizabeth. She was wearing a loose-fitting flowered dress—the kind Karen called a muu-muu—and holding a red purse the size of a small suitcase on her lap. Her mouth was moving continuously, chewing words as if they were gum.

He cleared his throat and said, "Can I help you?" It was what he'd said to his customers at ShopKo, and he felt strange for having said it now.

Elizabeth turned her moon face to him and abruptly, for the first time in his presence, went silent. But then she immediately started talking again. She was looking at him, but somehow he could tell she was still talking to herself.

"What's wrong?" he asked. But that, too, was a stupid question: she was smiling and every now and then a giggle broke into her babble. He stood watching her for a moment, not knowing what to do. Then he opened the door and said, "I'm sorry, but you'll have to leave." But she didn't move. She just opened her purse a crack, put her eye right down to the opening, and half giggled, half jabbered some strange phrase over and over. Then she suddenly snapped the purse shut and looked at him as if she thought he were trying to peek.

Larry didn't know what to say. "If you want to go somewhere," he finally said, "you picked the wrong car. This one doesn't even run."

Just then, Elizabeth's mother came huffing up the driveway in her housecoat. "Oh Mr. Watkins, you found her!" she said, trying to catch her breath. "I was so worried. I was just about to call the police." She came up beside Larry and looked in at Elizabeth. "You naughty girl!" she said. "You know you aren't supposed to go outside by yourself." Her scolding didn't seem to bother Elizabeth; she just sat there, chattering away happily and peeking every now and then in her purse.

The old woman turned back to Larry and, wiping her sweaty face with a handkerchief, said, "I don't know what's gotten into her, Mr. Watkins. I've been up and down the block looking for her, but I never thought to look in your"—she paused, as if she wasn't sure what to call it—"your car."

She went on talking, but Larry was only half listening to her. He was watching Elizabeth bounce up and down on the back seat like an excited child. "You know something," he interrupted the old woman. "I think she thinks she's going somewhere."

That night, Larry called Karen for the first time since she left. "Oh, it's you," she said.

"What's the matter?" he said. "Can't I call?"

"Yes, you can call. Just don't think you'll change my mind."

"I'm not calling about that," he said.

"Then what are you calling about?"

For a moment, he didn't answer. He was listening to Karen's mother, in the background, talking to Randy. She was using the high, sing-song voice grown-ups put on to talk to children. Larry strained to hear what she was saying, but all he could make out was "grow up big and strong." Then he realized Karen was on the phone in her parents' kitchen, and for a second he was standing where Karen was, looking across the room at the kitchen table, where her mother was sitting beside Randy's highchair, poking a spoonful of something at him. He felt a sudden ache, like hunger, in his stomach, and he gripped the telephone.

"You remember that retarded woman across the street?" he finally said.

"Of course I do. How long do you think I've been gone? Forty years?"

"Well, this morning she was sitting out in the Caddy. Her mother was looking everywhere for her. She was about to file a missing person report. And here she was, just sitting there in the back seat, smiling and jabbering like nothing in the world was wrong."

"If this is about that stupid car . . ."

"No. Really, I just wanted to call. I thought you'd want to hear what happened."

"Now why would I want to hear about that woman sitting in your worthless car?"

"I don't know," Larry said. And now that he thought about it, he didn't know why he'd wanted to call her and tell her. It all seemed so stupid now. Of course she wouldn't care. And why should *he* care?

In the background he heard his son say "Grandma" and suddenly he had to sit down. The last words Randy had said to him before he and Karen got on the bus were, "Grandma's gonna take me to the zoo."

Larry sat there, staring across the kitchen table at the sink where Karen used to give Randy a bath. He felt very tired all of a sudden. He wanted to put his head down on the table and go to sleep.

Then Karen said, "Are you still there?"

"Yes," he answered. "How's Randy?"

"He's fine. He's made friends with the neighbor's little four-year-old, and he's been playing with him all day in his sandbox."

"Tell him I'll build him a sandbox in the backyard if he wants."

"I told you, Larry. I'm not changing my mind."

"I know," he said. "I was just thinking about when he comes to visit. You know, on weekends or whatever."

"All right," she said. "I'm sorry. I didn't know what you meant. Listen, do you want to talk with him for a minute?"

Larry was quiet. Then he said, "No, I guess not."

"Are you all right?" Karen asked.

Larry stood and looked out the window at the garage. Then he said, "I've been working on the car. You should see it. It's looking pretty good. I hung the new drive shaft and split the door posts the weekend you left, then last week I finished bending the new side panels and installed the window frames."

"Larry," she said.

"It took me forever to run the wires from front to back," he went on. "Over fifty wires in all. But everything's electric now: the locks, the windows, you name it. And I just finished installing the extensions on the gas lines, brake lines, and exhaust. It's been a lot of work, but it's been worth it. I'm just about ready for the paint job. I've decided on a royal blue Corvette finish. I tell you, it's gonna be beautiful, Karen, really beautiful."

"Larry, I'm not going to listen to this."

"I'll take you for a ride in it when it's finished. You'll be the first one in it, you and Randy."

"Larry, I mean it."

"Okay," he said. "Okay. I'm sorry." Then they were silent for a long moment.

Finally, Karen said, "When will you understand? Even if you had done all of that, it wouldn't mean anything to me. I don't know why it's so important to you. Why can't you just let it go?"

"What do you mean, *if* I had done it?"

"You know what I mean."

"No, I don't," he said, his voice rising. "Why don't you tell me."

Karen sighed. "I don't want to sit here and fight with you, Larry. Randy's right here, and so's my mom."

"If you don't think I've been working on that car, you're wrong," he said. "Dead wrong."

"Okay. Okay. You've been working on it."

"Not just working on it, I'm damn near finished with it."

"I said okay. Don't get mad."

"I'm not mad. Who said I was mad?"

"Okay, you're not mad. You're not mad, and the limo's almost done. And I've changed my silly little mind and I'm not going to file for divorce after all."

"Don't talk to me that way."

"Why not? That's how you talk to me."

"You know what?" he said, pacing beside the table now. "You think you know everything. You think you're so smart. Well, you don't know shit. You understand? Not even *shit*."

"Larry, listen to yourself. You sound like—"

"You listen to yourself!" he shouted, then hung up the phone so hard it rang.

He stood there a moment, trembling, then went to the refrigerator and opened it. He stared inside for several minutes, not seeing anything, before he finally closed the door and went out to the garage. It was dark outside, and it'd be hard to work, even with utility lights, but he had to get busy. He had wasted too much time already. It was still terribly hot, and the weathermen were saying the heat might not break for another week, but he couldn't wait any longer. He took off his shirt, gripped the rear bumper, and pulled the back half of the Cadillac about six feet away from the front half. Then he began to align the frame, pausing every now and then to towel the sweat from his face and arms.

When he finished aligning the frame, he took an imprint of the end of the frame section, then stood and stretched his aching back. There was nothing else he could do now. He'd take the imprint to Hawker's the first thing in the morning, so they could begin building the frame extensions he needed. On his way back from Hawker's, he'd stop at Eriksen's Welding Supply and buy welding rods— about twenty pounds should do it—then swing by Vern's Sheet Metal to see about renting their break to bend the side panels. Hawker should have the extensions for him by the end of the week, so if he worked steadily he could be done welding the frame by the weekend. Then the next step would be installing the drive shaft. That was the trickiest part, according to the tour guide at the limousine factory, because the longer the drive shaft was, the greater the amount of torque it had to bear. Larry was planning to add at least one more hanger bearing, but still he was worried that the shaft would vibrate or even twist out of its supports. Several times he had imagined driving down the highway with Karen and Randy, the three of them talking and laughing as if nothing had ever been wrong between them, when all of a sudden the shaft would lurch out of the hanger bearings with a sound like the end of the world. Whenever this thought had come to him, he had forced himself to think of something else. But now he stood there between the two halves of the Cadillac and watched the shaft drag beneath the swerving car, spewing sparks.

The next morning, Larry was too exhausted to take the imprint down to Hawker's. He didn't even have the energy to watch TV, so he just lay on the couch and stared out the window. Birds flew by, lighting on the branches of the sycamore, and squirrels chattered and chased each other in the yard. He watched all this for a while, but he wasn't really seeing it. He was wondering what would have happened if he hadn't been born. Who would be living in this house, looking out the window? Who would Karen have married? And what would her son be like? The more he thought, the more he felt insubstantial, as if he had only been dreaming all these years that he existed. He looked around the room, and everything seemed simultaneously familiar and strange. He remembered how once, when he was a child, he had lain on the floor of his bedroom and imagined that the ceiling was the floor of an upside-down house and he was somehow stuck on the ceiling. Nothing was different—there was the same light fixture, the same posters on the walls, the same bed and carpet—but everything had changed.

Now he lay on the couch, watching the dust swirling in the light slanting through the window. It looked like snow. He watched it fall for a long time, wondering if it would ever stop. It didn't. It kept falling, but as it fell out of the light, it disappeared.

Then he held his hand up to the light and turned it back and forth. *I'm here*, he thought. *I'm alive and I'm here.*

Later that morning, the doorbell rang. It was Elizabeth's mother, her face a knot of worry. "I'm afraid she's in your car again, Mr. Watkins, and I can't get her out."

Larry was dizzy from standing suddenly after lying down so long, and he hung onto the doorjamb. In the bright sunlight, the old lady's wrinkled face looked as if it had been burned, and it occurred to him that that's what aging was: a gradual kind of fire that ate your flesh. He shivered, even though the air coming through the screen door was oppressively hot.

"I'm sorry to bother you," she said, and took a step back down the stairs. "If this isn't a good time . . ."

Then Larry realized he had been staring at her for some time without speaking. "Excuse me," he apologized. "I just woke up, and I'm a little groggy. I'll be happy to help you."

He slipped on his tennis shoes and followed the old woman out to the garage where, as before, Elizabeth was sitting in the back seat with her purse on her lap. But this time she wasn't just jabbering; she was singing. Larry couldn't recognize the song, if it was a song. He remembered how Randy would make up nonsense songs, and it occurred to him that children—and maybe retarded people, too—didn't know that words existed. Maybe they thought words were only sounds, meaningless noises people made back and forth, to pass the day. Or maybe it was the other way around and they thought every sound was a word. And maybe they were right, maybe every sound *was* a word, and they weren't speaking nonsense after all.

Elizabeth's mother said, "I've tried everything, but I can't get her to budge. She can be very stubborn, you know."

Larry opened the door and said, "Elizabeth. It's time for you to go home." She stopped singing for a second and looked at him, then opened her purse a crack and peeked in. Then she smiled and started singing again.

Her mother shook her head. "Who knows what all she's got in that purse this time. Yesterday I found my missing bottle of perfume in there, and her toothbrush, and a pair of socks. I'd been looking for that perfume for a week."

Larry turned to her. "When was the last time you took her somewhere? You know, on a trip."

"Oh, once in a while I take her with me to the grocery store. And every other Sunday we go to church. But otherwise—well, you can see how much trouble she can be, and I'm not strong enough to make her behave."

"Yes," Larry said, "I can see that." Then he looked in at Elizabeth and said, "Where're you headed today?" Elizabeth babbled excitedly and clapped her hands. "No kidding?" Larry said. "Me, too." Then he climbed into the front seat and took the wheel in his hands.

"Mr. Watkins?" the old lady said, clasping the collar of her dress with a bony hand.

"Don't worry," he answered. "I'll have her back before lunchtime."

Every morning after that, Elizabeth spent a few hours in the car, and each day her purse got a little fuller until finally she couldn't close it anymore. Eventually, Larry began to get up before she did, and he'd be waiting in the limo when she crossed the street, chattering and waggling her arms. She'd sit in the back and he'd sit behind the wheel, watching her in the rearview mirror as she bounced up and down on the seat and pointed out the window at the world passing by. For hours at a time, he didn't think about Karen or Randy or the threatening letters from the bank and electric company. He was not happy, but he was not unhappy either. He was Elizabeth's chauffeur, nothing more, and he just sat there, his mind empty. And it wasn't until after they'd finished their drive and he'd helped her across the street to her house that he would come back to who and where he was. When that happened, he'd stand there a minute, in her yard or in the street or on his steps, before he could bear to enter his house.

Toward the middle of August, a man came to serve divorce papers on Larry. He started up the walk, then heard strange noises coming from the garage. Crossing the yard to the driveway, he saw the rear end of a car sticking out of the garage. Then, as he reached the door, he saw that the car had been sawn in half and there were two people sitting in it. "What the hell?" he said. He called out Larry's name, but Larry didn't seem to notice; he just kept looking out the windshield at the garage wall. He was silent, but the woman in the back seat was jabbering in some strange language the process server couldn't understand. But Larry seemed to understand. He nodded as she spoke, said something back to her, then turned the wheel carefully to the left, as if rounding a dangerous curve.

Freeze

AT FIRST Freeze Harris thought Nam was a crazy nightmare, an upside-down place where you were supposed to do everything that was forbidden back in the world, but after a while it was the world that seemed unreal. Cutting ears off dead NVA had become routine; stocking shelves at Kroger's seemed something he'd only dreamed. Then, on a mission in the Iron Triangle, Freeze stepped on a Bouncing Betty that didn't go off and nothing seemed real anymore. It was like he'd stepped out of Nam when he stepped on the mine. And now he wasn't anywhere.

The day after Freeze stepped on the mine, the new brown-bar reported for duty. His name was Reynolds, and from the moment he arrived at Lai Khe, he had it in for Freeze. Freeze had just come in off the line that morning, and he was stumbling drunk outside the bunny club, wearing only his bush hat, sunglasses, and Jockey shorts. He had a bottle of Carling Black Label in one hand and a fragmentation grenade in the other. He was standing there, swaying back and forth, when Reynolds came up to him, his jungle fatigues starched and razor-creased, and stuck his square, government-issue jaw into Freeze's face. "What the fuck are you doing, soldier?"

Freeze looked at the brown bar on Reynolds' collar and saluted with the grenade. "Drinking, sir. Beer, sir."

"I'm not blind, Private. I'm talking about the frag."

Freeze looked at the grenade. He had pulled the pin after his first six-pack. If he let go of the firing lever, he'd have only four and a half seconds to make out his will. *I, Mick Harris, being of unsound mind and body . . .* He laughed.

There were red blotches on the lieutenant's white face now. "What's so funny, hand job?"

Freeze laughed again. He closed his eyes, woozy, and shrugged his shoulders. "You," he said. "Me."

Reynolds stiffened. "I'm ordering you to dispose of that frag immediately and safely."

"Can't," Freeze said. "Beer tastes like piss without it." He raised the bottle to his lips.

When he lowered it, the lieutenant had disappeared. Freeze looked around but didn't see him anywhere. Maybe he'd never been there. Maybe he'd imagined it all. He took another long drink from the bottle, concentrating on his sweaty fingers gripping the firing lever. His hand was starting to go numb. It was almost like it was dissolving, disappearing. When he finished his drink, he looked at his hand. It was still there.

As he tilted the bottle back to take another drink, he heard someone say, "Here's the son of a bitch." He squinted toward the voice. The brown-bar was back, a sneer on his face. There was another face too, but this one was grinning. It was an MP. He had a harelip that made his grin look like it was splitting his face. Freeze imagined his face cracking like an egg and laughed.

Then the MP lunged at Freeze, grabbing his hand and twisting it behind his back. The sudden pain made Freeze groan and drop the beer in his other hand. While he looked down at the bottle foaming on the red dirt, the MP pried his fingers open. Then the pain was gone and Freeze looked up. The MP stuck the grenade in Freeze's face and grinned. "My turn to play with this," he said.

Reynolds said, "Cut that shit. Just toss the frag out on the perimeter, then take this soldier to the stockade and let him sleep it off. I'll deal with him in the morning." Then he turned and strode away.

Frigging brown-bar, Freeze thought, and imagined him stepping on a mine and blowing into a hundred pieces.

Only later, after the harelip had hauled him to the stockade and asked him his name, company, platoon, and squad, did Freeze find out that the brown-bar was his new platoon leader. "Your ass is gonna be grass come morning," the MP said, laughing. "Reynolds, he's your new LT." But Freeze didn't care. What could the bastard do to him? Send him to Nam? All he wanted to do was sleep. Sleep and dream. When he woke up, everything would be clear again, everything would be back to normal.

But the next morning he felt worse. He'd been dreaming about a mummy he'd seen in a museum when he was a kid. The mummy was the color of caramel, and in his dream he'd broken off one of the toes and taken a bite. Then a gum-chewing guard woke him, and for a moment he thought the guard had taken a bite too. "Feeling all bright-eyed and bushy-tailed this morning, Private?" another voice said, and Freeze turned toward it: Reynolds, grinning.

The lieutenant tossed some wrinkled fatigues onto Freeze's cot. "Get up and get dressed," he said. "You've got a party to go to, and you're the guest of honor." Then he told Freeze that he and Konieczny were to report to the privies by 0700 for shit-burning detail.

Freeze sat up slowly, his head heavy and aching. "*Konieczny?*"

he said. Konieczny was the big, red-haired recruit just off the bus from Bien Hoa. It was bad enough to put him in the stockade, but to treat him like that twink Konieczny . . . He'd spent ten months in-country—*ten fucking months*—and he'd walked point for the first three. Nobody in his company had walked point that long, and they gave him a badge just for having survived. And now this new brown-bar was treating him like a goddamn twink.

"That's right. Since he's a new recruit, I thought you could teach him some of the finer points of shit-burning. Now chop chop," Reynolds said, then turned and left.

"You heard the man," the guard said, then went back to chewing his gum.

Freeze watched the guard chew. *Eat death*, he thought, and smiled to himself. *Chew that gristle down.*

He tried to stand then, but his head was pounding so hard he sat back on the cot with a moan. He stayed there, dizzy, for a moment, then stood slowly and dressed. Each movement made his head throb.

When Freeze finished tying his boots, the guard escorted him back to barracks. Though it was still early, it was already so hot that Freeze's shirt had soaked through by the time they got there. The guard said, "Enjoy your party," and left. Freeze opened the screen door and went inside. It wasn't much cooler in the hootch. All the men were shirtless, but their chests were still wet with sweat. Some of them had pulled their footlockers out into the middle of the wooden plank floor and were sitting on them playing cards and drinking Cokes or smoking joints. A few were lying on their racks reading magazines or letters. Others were talking and laughing about some photograph they were passing around. When they looked up and saw Freeze, they went quiet for a moment. Then Jackson put down his cards and said, "You okay, man?"

That's what he'd said after Freeze had stepped on the mine. He'd come up to him, put his hand on his shoulder, and said, "Hey man, you okay?" Over and over, "You okay?" When Freeze had finally been able to answer, he told Jackson to fuck off, he was all right, leave him alone. But Jackson didn't back off. None of them did. For the rest of the patrol, they all stayed close to him, thinking they were safe if they were around him. He had the magic, they said, the luck. He wasn't going to get greased. The mine had proved that. So they stuck close to Freeze until finally he turned his M-16 on them and said he'd shoot the next mother who came near.

Now Freeze looked at Jackson, then at the others. Once he had been closer to these guys than to anybody in his whole life. But ever since he'd stepped on the mine they had seemed like strangers. He felt like he'd walked into someone else's barracks, someone else's life.

"Yeah," he said to Jackson. "I'm okay." Then he crossed over to his rack and pulled off his drenched shirt. Kneeling down, he started to dig through his bamboo footlocker.

"I hear you and Konieczny are going to a party," Clean Machine said, then laughed. "Some people have all the luck."

Freeze looked at him, but he didn't say anything.

Duckwalk sat down on Freeze's rack. "I hope you're doing all right," he said. "We been worried about you, bro."

Freeze didn't answer. He was trying to remember what he was looking for in his footlocker. Then it came to him: cotton. He found some in the neck of an aspirin bottle and tore off two chunks. Then he stood and turned to Konieczny, who was waiting in front of his rack, smiling uneasily. "What're you laughing at, twink?" he said. Konieczny just stood there, looking confused.

"Ain't nobody laughing," Boswell said, and pushed his Stetson back on his head. "Ain't nothing funny here." Then he looked at Jackson. "You want to finish this hand, pardner? 'Cause if you don't I'll be plenty happy to pick up that pot."

Jackson looked at Freeze, his forehead creased. "You still with us?" he asked.

"What's it to you?" Freeze said.

Jackson looked down and shook his head, then he picked up his cards and turned back to the game.

Freeze went outside then and stood in the heat, his head pounding. He wanted to go back to sleep. Maybe when he woke up he would be Mick again, not Freeze, and the mine would be just a bad dream.

In a moment, Konieczny joined him and they marched in silence up the hill to the latrine, each of them humping a can of diesel fuel. When they got there, Freeze stuffed the cotton up his nostrils, glaring at Konieczny all the while. Then they lifted the shelter off its blocks, exposing the fifty-five gallon drums cut in half, and started to soak the shit with fuel.

"Jesus," Konieczny said. "This is number ten."

Freeze didn't say anything; he was thinking how much he hated Reynolds for making him do this. If the son of a bitch was here right now, he'd throw him into the shit barbecue. Lieutenant Crispy Critter. He smiled as he poured the fuel into the latrine.

"Make that ten thousand," Konieczny said, his hand over his nose and mouth.

Though it was still early, the day was so hot and humid that the air seemed too thick to breathe. Freeze was breathing through his open mouth because of the cotton in his nose, and it felt like he was suffocating. His head throbbed and his stomach felt queasy. Then the smell of the diesel fumes and the shit suddenly penetrated the cotton and made him drop to his knees. With a noise like a bark, he vomited onto the red dirt between his trembling palms.

"You all right?" Konieczny asked, leaning over him.

Freeze wiped his mouth and looked up at Konieczny's face, its freckles and peachfuzz and acne. The twink would be lucky if he lasted a week in the bush. Freeze could see him tripping a mine and blowing into the air, his body cut in half. He remembered how Perkins had looked after he triggered a Bouncing Betty. He'd had

21

his wet intestines in his hands, and he was trying to put them back in. Or had Freeze just dreamed that?

He looked away, squinting in the sun. "Fuck you," he answered.

"Just trying to help," the kid said. He shrugged his shoulders and turned back to the work.

Freeze stood, his legs quivering. He thought about saying he was sorry, but then he'd have to explain and he didn't know how to explain or even what to explain. So they finished soaking the shit without talking, then dropped matches on it. Black smoke curdled out of the pit, and the stench made them gag. Standing there beside the blaze, his eyes burning, head swimming, Freeze almost threw up again. And later, back in the hootch, he lay on his rack, the stink of the burning shit still thick in his nostrils, and heaved his guts into a C-rats can. His heart was beating fast, like it did when they were in a fire fight. What had happened? He'd been a strack soldier for ten months, an assistant squad leader—leader of the first fire team—for the past four, ever since C.B. got zapped. And now he was a shit-burner. God, how he hated that frigging brown-bar.

Hating the lieutenant made him feel better than he had since he'd stepped on the mine; it made things seem more real, more logical. So he stoked his hate, made it grow. Everything was Reynolds' fault. Reynolds was the evil heart of it all. If it wasn't for him, he'd be happy now, he'd be one of the guys again, nothing would have changed. The bastard was worse than Charlie.

Lying there on his canvas cot, Freeze imagined Reynolds walking point through knee-high brush. Then he saw him stop dead. He'd felt something under his boot. For a second, stupidly, Reynolds thought it was a scorpion, or a rock, but then he felt the pin sink and he knew it was the metal prong of a Bouncing Betty. Before he could move, or even think, the mine flew up out of the ground with a pop. Reynolds closed his eyes and covered his head with his hands, and for a moment, a moment that stretched out until it was outside of time, he waited for the explosion of light, the thundering roar, the hail of shrapnel. Then the moment ended and the Bouncing Betty fell back at his feet, dead. The main charge hadn't gone off. Reynolds opened his eyes and stood there for several minutes, panting hard, the sweat rolling off his face and dripping onto the mine, his eyes staring into ozone. *Hey*, his men would say later, *you should have seen the brown-bar freeze.*

Freeze planned his revenge all afternoon. Then, an hour or so before dusk, he saw Reynolds go into the officers' club. After waiting a few minutes to be sure he wasn't coming back out, he snuck into Reynolds' quarters. He had planned to fire a single pistol shot into his pillow and leave, but once he was there, that plan seemed too dangerous, even crazy. He had to do something, though, so he stole the two officer-grade steaks Reynolds had in his refrigerator. He stuffed them inside his shirt and left, almost giddy. He could just see the look on Reynolds' face when he saw the steaks were missing.

Back in the hootch, Freeze put the smaller steak up for auction. He stood on his footlocker and dangled the slab in front of his squad. "What am I bid for this hunk of heaven?" he said.

Duckwalk was sitting on his rack, cleaning an AK-47 he'd souvenired from an NVA. He shook his head. "The LT's gonna fuck you, Freeze," he said.

"You'll have his steaks for supper, but he'll have your ass for breakfast," Jackson agreed. "He's gonna know you swiped his meat." He took another drag on his joint and went back to playing solitaire on his footlocker.

Everybody was trying to act uninterested, but Freeze knew better. He knew how long it had been since anybody'd had a steak. To them, even the warm Cokes they got every stand-down were bennies.

"Let's start the bidding at a bag of el primo no-stem, no-seed, shall we?" he said and grinned. He was having fun. He had crossed over the edge of hatred and now he was having fun. He could barely keep from laughing.

"Are you nuts?" said McKeown. "We buy that hot cow and we're in as much trouble as you."

"Smoke my pole," Boswell said.

"Shit," Clean Machine said. "I wouldn't give one joint for your sister and your mother both."

But before long, McKeown offered a pack of Park Lanes and soon they were all bidding. When it was over, Clean had shelled out four packs of Park Lanes and a handful of military payment certificates for the steak. Freeze stashed his loot under the floorboard beneath his rack, then ditty-bopped out to the perimeter where nobody could see him and hunkered down in some brush to broil his steak. He lit a tin of Sterno and set it over a little stove he'd made by puncturing an empty C-rats can. Then he started to broil the steak on a steel plate he'd ripped off the back of a Claymore mine.

Smelling the steak browning on the plate, he forgot the stench of the burning shit for the first time that day. He leaned back on one elbow, lit a Park Lane, and inhaled deeply, holding the smoke in his lungs. As he smoked, he looked out over the brush at the lead-colored sky and tried to daydream about going back to the world. He imagined he was back in Little Rock, lying on a lounge chair beside his apartment pool, catching some rays and checking out the talent. But the daydream began to unravel as soon as it started. First he couldn't remember what his pool had looked like. Then he wasn't even sure whether he'd had a pool at Cromwell Court or if that was earlier, at the Cantrell Apartments. And the girls that strolled by in their bikinis were faceless, vague. He tried to remember Mary Ellen, the girl he'd dated the fall before he enlisted, but nothing would come to him. He wasn't sure of the color of her eyes or hair, the sound of her voice. He laughed. Then he listened to himself laugh. It was such a strange sound. He wondered why he'd never noticed how strange it was. He tried to remember Mary Ellen's laugh, but it was no use. Ever since he'd come to Nam he'd been forgetting things, and now almost everything was gone. And what he did remember seemed more like something he'd overheard in a bar, some dim, muffled conversation. He couldn't have seen Perkins holding his plastic yellow guts, or C.B.'s brains in his mouth, the top of his skull turned to pulp. He couldn't have seen these things. It was impossible. Wasn't Perkins transferred to another company? Hadn't C.B. gone back to the world?

By the time Freeze finally remembered to turn over the steak, it had burned black.

After lights out, a heavy monsoon rain began to beat against the ponchos nailed on the outside of the hootch. The wind whipped the water against the green plastic, battering the hootch like incoming.

Then it *was* incoming. Duckwalk sat up in the rack next to Freeze's. "You hear that?" he asked.

Freeze sat up, his poncho liner wrapped around him.

"Not tonight, Charlie," Jackson moaned, "I'm having me a wet dream."

They listened as the mortars walked in closer and closer. At first there was only a distant pop, then a closer thud. Then they heard the whistling of a round and the roar of an explosion.

"Shit," Freeze said. And he and the rest of the men scrambled out of their racks, grabbing their M-16s, and double-timed in their skivvies out into the cold pounding rain. Through the rain's thick odor of rot, they could smell the sharp scents of gunpowder and cordite. On the perimeter of the camp, M-79 grenade launchers and mortars were thumping into a sky green with star flares, punctuating the nonstop sentence of an M-16 on rock-'n'-roll.

In the platoon bunker, they huddled behind the wet sandbags, shivering, staring out at the dark. Konieczny was next to Freeze.

"Are they gonna come through the wire?" he asked. When a star flare burst, his face turned green, a Martian's, and Freeze felt the urge to laugh. Then he heard the whistle of an incoming round. He ducked and waited for the burst. It seemed to take forever. Looking around, he saw that everyone was still, as if they'd been frozen. He remembered the game he'd played as a kid back in Arkansas. Statues. It was like they were playing Statues.

Then the shell exploded nearby, raining shrapnel into the bunker, and everybody came alive again. Somebody started screaming.

Reynolds stood up at his end of the bunker. "Who's down?"

Everybody looked around. But no one was hurt. Then the screaming started again. It was coming from outside the bunker.

"I'm dying!" the man yelled. "Help me!"

Before anyone could say anything, Reynolds had crawled out of the bunker and started to run in a crouch toward a man lying in the mud halfway between the second platoon hootch and bunker. Under the light of the star flares, Freeze watched the brown-bar drag the man toward their bunker. For a second he admired Reynolds for rescuing the soldier when he could have ordered someone else to do it, but then he felt the comforting return of hate. *The hotdog*, he thought. *He's bucking for goddamn Eagle Scout.*

The moment Reynolds made it back, they heard the whistle of another mortar and ducked, holding their breaths until it exploded. Then they looked up.

Someone shined his flashlight on the man. "Jesus H. Christ," Reynolds said then, and turned away, disgusted. The man was all right. He hadn't been hit at all. Still, he was moaning as if he were dying.

"Save me," the soldier pleaded. "Don't let me die. I don't want to die." It was clear that he wasn't talking to anybody there. He was staring up at the sky, his eyes blank as milk glass, and whimpering. And he wasn't even a twink. He'd been in the bush long enough to get a bad case of jungle rot. It had invaded his face, and though he'd tried to hide it by growing a scruffy beard, it made his skin look raw.

They told him he was okay, but he kept on moaning and crying. Even after the mortars stopped falling and the machine guns faded to random bursts, he would not stop.

The rest of the men looked away, embarrassed, but Freeze couldn't take his eyes off him.

The next morning, the other soldiers were laughing about the man who thought he was wounded, calling him a snuffy, a wuss, and praising Reynolds for risking his butt to save him. They even had a nickname for Reynolds now. "Man, did you see the look he gave that poge?" Jackson had said. "It was righteous rabid." And it stuck. All the while they prepared for inspection, the men talked about Righteous Rabid and The Wuss. A week before, Freeze would have joined in. But he wasn't one of them anymore.

At inspection, Reynolds stopped in front of Freeze and poked him in the gut with his finger. "Private Harris," he said, "you look like you've put on a couple of pounds since yesterday." He looked Freeze in the eye. "Maybe you had an extra helping of ham and mothers? Or maybe the entire platoon gave you their cookies?"

Freeze stood there a moment. For some reason he was suddenly sleepy. He wanted to lie down and go to sleep right there on the floor of the hootch.

"I'm talking to you, Private," Reynolds said.

Freeze just stood there. He was so tired he didn't even have the energy to lie.

"So you did do it," Reynolds said. Then he put his face in Freeze's. "I'm going to report this little incident to Captain Arnold, and I'm going to recommend that you receive an Article 15. If I have my way, he'll bust your ass to E-1." Reynolds sneered. "But until then you can party. How does filling sandbags sound for starters?"

A mortar shell had blasted through the first layer of sandbags during the attack and ripped into the second layer, spilling sand like guts. It would take hours to fill enough sandbags to repair the bunker, and it was going to be another hundred and ten degree day. Already the sun was burning off the puddles left by the rain.

Freeze stared at the blue vein that popped out on Reynolds' forehead, between his eyes, a perfect target. "It sounds like shit," he heard someone say. It was a second before he realized he was the one who said it.

Reynolds stiffened.

"What did you say, poge?"

Freeze said, "Cut me some slack."

Reynolds' eyes narrowed. "Maybe one Article 15 isn't enough for you, Harris. Maybe you'd like another."

Freeze stared at him. He was trying to hate him, trying to recapture the way he'd felt when he stole the steaks, but he couldn't get it back. He wanted it back desperately, but it wouldn't come. After a moment he looked down.

"No, I didn't think you'd want any more," Reynolds said then, stepping back and smiling. "I figured you'd had enough."

The rest of that morning, Freeze filled sandbags in the dizzying heat, his back and shoulders aching, while a fatass MP named Hulsey stood by the bunker, throwing his walnut baton into the air and catching it. He was trying to see how many times he could spin the baton and still catch it. So far his record was six revolutions. Whenever he dropped the baton, he'd say "Uncle fucking Ho" and spit. Freeze stood, stretching his stiff back, and watched the MP fling the baton. He shook his head. He'd come halfway around the world to watch a man toss a baton into the air and try to catch it. And the MP had made the same trip to watch a man shovel sand. Freeze wanted to tell him how crazy it was, maybe suggest they go get a beer, but the MP caught the baton and said, "*Seven.* A new record! Let's hear it for the boy from Brooklyn." Freeze turned back to his work.

He finished repairing the bunker just before noon. He thought the brown-bar was done with him then, but after lunch, Reynolds gave him more scut work to do. He mopped the barracks, unloaded ammo crates from a deuce-and-a-half truck, and then helped carry the wounded from medevac helicopters, humping stretchers down the metal ramp to the deck, where medics sorted the living from the dead. He was so exhausted from working in the heat that he could barely stand in the prop wash of the helicopters. He staggered in the hot wind, gravel swarming around him, stinging like hornets, and felt his hatred for Reynolds rise almost to madness. He knew Reynolds was just making an example of him, using him to prove to the others that he was in charge and wouldn't take any shit, and he knew he'd back off as soon as he felt he'd made his point. But Freeze didn't care. He still hated him. The bastard had treated him like a dead man's turd ever since he came. He'd embarrassed him in front of his best friends, he'd turned them against him. He could hear the men now, talking and laughing about Righteous Rabid and Freeze. Well, he'd give them something to talk about. When they got out in the bush, he'd frag the son of a bitch. This decision made him feel suddenly calm, even happy, but then he saw Reynolds lying dead on the jungle floor, his eyes open to nothing, his face mottled with shadows cast by the sunlight flickering through the trees, and everything was as confused as a dream again because Reynolds was wearing Freeze's fatigues and he was smiling. Grinning. Almost laughing. Freeze stood there in the prop wash until his partner yelled from the chopper's cargo bay for him to hurry up and give him a hand.

A few minutes later, as he bent to pick up his end of a stretcher, he saw that one of the grunt's legs had been blown off just below the knee and that the other was terribly mangled. Someone had laid the severed leg on top of him. He had his arms around it, holding it to his chest, and he was staring off somewhere, a slight smile frozen on his lips, as if he'd just heard something mildly funny.

"Heavy fucker, ain't he?" Freeze's partner said, as they hoisted the stretcher.

The next day the stand-down ended and the company was sent back out on line. They stood inspection, marched to the air field, climbed aboard the choppers and flew north over the jungle, finally setting down in the brush and bamboo of Tay Ninh province. Freeze was glad to be in the bush; he'd rather be in the shit, where all you had to worry about was someone greasing you, than in camp, where poge officers like Reynolds policed your every move. He figured that Reynolds would let up on him now, but if he didn't, Freeze would pick his moment and frag his ass.

Reynolds didn't let up. The first day after they'd finished carving Fire Base Molly out of the jungle, stripping the foliage down to the bare dirt, digging bunkers, and stringing coils of concertina wire around the perimeter, he dispatched Freeze, Konieczny, and Clean to secure a helicopter supply drop for a tank column—three men to defend thousands of gallons of diesel fuel and tons of ammo.

"One dink with a hand grenade could blow the whole damn drop to Saigon," Freeze complained, though he didn't really care.

Reynolds looked at him. "The tank column is due at 1900 hours. Saddle up." Then he turned and walked away.

Freeze raised his hand and sighted down his index finger at the lieutenant's back. *Bang.*

Duckwalk turned to him, his thumbs hooked behind the silver buckle of the NVA belt he'd souvenired from a sniper. "Relax, bro," he said. "He's just the Army. What you expect him to do—be your friend?"

Freeze didn't say anything. He shouldered his pack and headed out toward the supply drop with Konieczny and Clean. When they got there, Konieczny sat on one of the crates and radioed back to

Reynolds. Freeze broke open another crate. "Chocolate milk," he said, taking out a carton and shaking his head. "Chocolate fucking milk."

"What's your problem, Freeze?" Clean said. "I'm getting sick of this shit. We're all getting sick of it."

Freeze looked at Clean. Then he opened the carton and took a drink. When he finished, he wiped his mouth with the back of his hand. "Whatever you do," he said, "don't let this milk fall into enemy hands."

Then he turned and humped off into a stand of bamboo a couple of hundred meters away and crawled down into a crater left by a mortar shell. He lay there, smoking a Park Lane, and thought about greasing Reynolds. He had to be careful; if he got caught, they'd put him in Long Binh Jail and the only world he'd go back to would be Leavenworth. But even that might be worth it. He imagined Reynolds face-down on the ground, his brains leaking out his open mouth. As soon as Reynolds was dead, he could rest. Everything would make sense again and he'd be at peace. He took out another joint and smoked it. The sun bore down on him, its heat a heavy weight, and soon he fell asleep.

He didn't wake until he felt the ground tremble and heard the steel rumble of the tanks. The sun was hovering over the edge of the horizon, staining the countryside a dusty red. Climbing out of the crater, he sauntered back to the supply drop. He came up to Konieczny and Clean just as the tanks rolled over the rise.

Clean looked at him. "Thanks for your fucking help."

Konieczny looked down the road and didn't say anything.

Freeze didn't know Clean had reported him until the next day, when Reynolds led the platoon on a reconnaissance-in-force. They humped through the jungle all morning, sweating under their packs; then, toward midday, they smelled shit cooking in the heat. It had to be an NVA camp. Through a stand of bamboo, they spotted a row of bunkers. Reynolds ordered Freeze's fire team to go in first, and they approached in a cloverleaf pattern. But the camp was abandoned. Bombers had attacked it, probably no more than a week before, and there were tank-sized craters everywhere. In a few places, the ground was still white from the phosphorous the spotter plane had dropped to give the B-52s their target. There was no sign of the NVA anywhere. Still, Reynolds ordered Freeze to check out a bunker that hadn't been caved in by the bombs.

"It's crawling with fire ants," Freeze said. "There's no gooks in there."

"I said check it out, Harris."

"Why me?" Freeze said.

Reynolds glared at him. "Yesterday I gave you a direct order, and you subverted it. It will not happen again."

Freeze looked at Konieczny, then at Clean. Clean crossed his arms on his chest and looked back.

So Freeze climbed down and checked the bunker out, and when he came scrambling out a moment later, the ants were all over him. He jumped up and down, swatting and swiping at the red sons of bitches, while the men laughed at him.

"You bastard," Freeze said to Reynolds. "You motherfucking bastard. I'm not going to eat any more of your shit."

"Oh yes you will," Reynolds said. "You'll eat it. You'll lick your plate clean, and you'll ask for more."

Freeze stood there, breathing hate, and stared at Reynolds, an animal snarl on his face. He hated him more than he'd ever hated the NVA. He hated him more than the heat and the jungle, the leeches and mosquitoes, the monsoon rains, the smells of sulfur and shit and death, more than his sixty-pound pack, the blisters on his shoulders, the wet socks, the jungle rot and immersion foot, more than the lizards that cried *fuck you, fuck you* in the night, the thump of mortars, the booby traps, more even than the mine that hadn't gone off.

"That's a negative," Freeze said, and before Reynolds could move, he snapped the bolt of his M-16, chambering a round, and shoved the flash suppressor into his belly, just under his ribs. The blood was drumming in his temples.

Reynolds sucked in a breath. The men stepped back. "Holy shit," Konieczny said.

"Take it easy, bro," Jackson said. "Everybody's watching. You don't want to do nothing when everybody's watching."

Freeze ignored him. He stared at Reynolds. Reynolds opened his mouth to say something, but no words came out. He closed and opened it again. Sweat began to bead on his upper lip. Freeze focused on one of the beads, and waited for it to slide down his lip and break. But it didn't move. It hung there, as if time had stopped, as if there were no more time.

Then everything went out of Freeze. What was he so angry about? It didn't mean anything anymore. It didn't seem real. Nothing seemed real. The drop of sweat. The circle of men staring at him like he was a gook. Reynolds. He looked around at the craters that surrounded them. They could be on the moon. He lowered his rifle and sat down in the red dust, suddenly dizzy. His hands were trembling.

Then Reynolds blinked and swallowed hard. He looked around him and finally found words. "Konieczny," he said, his voice shaking slightly, "get on the horn to HQ. We need to call in a chopper to remove Private Harris to the stockade."

Konieczny said, "Yes sir" and began to call headquarters.

Reynolds looked down at Freeze then and, squaring his shoulders, said, in a voice that shook now more with anger than fear, "Get this son of a bitch out of my sight. Get him out of here before I kill him."

But Freeze didn't hear him. He wasn't there. He had stepped on the mine and he was rising into the air, twisting and turning in the bursting light for one last peaceful second.

Beautiful Ohio

T HIS COUPLE came in and took a table in the far corner, where
the shadows almost swallow up the candlelight. That's how I knew
they were lovers, not father and daughter. That, and the way he
held her hands and leaned over the table, his eyes never leaving her
face all the while he talked to her. He was old enough to be her
father, though: at least forty, maybe forty-five. But his hair was that
sort of premature gray that somehow makes a man seem younger
instead of older, and he had the tan of a movie star or a doctor. He
was wearing a white sportjacket and a navy knit shirt open at the
neck, and he had two silver rings on his left hand. The girl was just
a girl, blonde, like they always are at that age, at least for a summer.
She wasn't wearing any make-up that I could see, but then who
needs it when you're that young? I'd seen the dress she was
wearing—one with a lacy yoke and puffy sleeves—in the window of
Cohn's, so I knew it was expensive. I wondered if he bought it for
her, or if her daddy did.

Of course I thought right away about Roy and that high school
dropout of his. How could I help it? I try not to think about him,
but what can I do? Lenny tells me to forget Roy and marry him, but

it's not that easy. We were married sixteen years. His new wife was still crawling around in diapers when we walked down the aisle.

Just thinking about Roy took the breath out of me. I can be going along, doing my job, happy, not thinking about anything, and then all of a sudden I think about him. I should expect it by now, I suppose, but I'm always surprised. That night, the thought of him hit me so hard I wanted to go home, make myself a drink, and climb into a tub full of soapy water. But I couldn't go home. I had two more hours left on my shift, and besides, Lenny was there, and he'd want to know what was wrong. I thought of asking Tia to take their table for me, but she already had a full section and I didn't want to have to explain. So I took two menus out of the rack and started through the imitation arbor toward their table.

I don't know why, but somehow I just knew they were talking about his wife. Maybe it was the way they were leaning over the table, like conspirators, or maybe it was the way they were smiling. I don't know. But as I walked toward them, I could almost hear him saying *the old bitch*, just like Roy did when he introduced me to his dropout after the divorce: *I'd like you to meet the old bitch.* The old bitch. *Me.* She didn't look a day over sixteen, but I didn't say anything. I had something all planned, some comment about how Roy had finally gotten the baby he'd always wanted, but when I got my chance, I couldn't say it. I just waved my hand, like I was dismissing two children. Then I watched Roy's green Pontiac speed down the street. That was almost two years ago now, but sometimes I still find myself imagining that old car driving up to our house and Roy stepping out, a sheepish smile on his face, and saying, "Honey, I'm home." I don't love him anymore—it isn't that. If he asked me to marry him again, I'd say no. I just want him to come home, to say he'd been wrong to leave.

Then I thought about Lenny, sitting home alone all these nights, waiting for me to give him an answer, and I started to feel so trembly I stopped at an empty table near theirs and pretended to straighten the placemats and silverware while I got ahold of myself. I was close enough then to really hear what they were saying, and I almost had to laugh, I'd been such a fool. They weren't talking about his wife, or divorce, at all. They were talking about *clay-eaters.*

"What they do," the man was saying, "is they mix the clay with tomato soup. They call it river beans."

The girl shook her head. "I can't believe it. I could understand it if they were starving or something, but why would anyone *want* to eat clay?"

"They crave it. No one knows why, but they do. If one of them moves away from the river, they crave it so bad their relatives have to mail them packages of it."

"Care packages full of dirt," the girl laughed.

I'd been a perfect fool and I knew it. Still, when I finally went up to their table, I felt my stomach turn over the way it would if I were waiting on Roy and his new wife. "Hello," I said, my voice wavering a little, and set the menus on the red-and-white checked tablecloth. "My name is Gloria, and I'll be serving you this evening."

The girl flicked a strand of blonde away from her eyes and smiled at me. "Tell me, do you have river beans tonight?" Then she and the man laughed.

"You'll have to excuse us," the man said. "We've been talking about a TV special I saw, about these people in Kentucky who eat clay."

"Real clay," the girl added, like I didn't understand.

"That's right," the man went on. "They dig it up out of the banks of the Ohio River and eat it. Not just poor people either: bankers, doctors, you name it."

He smiled.

I can't explain why, but right then I decided I had to give Lenny his answer. I couldn't wait another night.

"I'll be back in a minute to take your orders," I said, then turned and went back to the kitchen. Edward, our cook, was spreading pepperoni slices on a pizza crust. He took one look at me and said, "Hey, Sunshine, what's the problem?"

"Nothing," I said.

"Sure," he said. "I can see that." Then he wiped his hands on his apron like he was going to give me a hug and make everything all right.

"Don't touch me," I said. "I'm fine."

When Lenny and I first met, I didn't know what to think of him. He wasn't anything like Roy. Roy was short, like me, and burly with a coarse black beard, and Lenny's tall and lanky and he has a dirty brown mustache that he chews whenever he's nervous, which is almost always. Roy never said what he was thinking much, but Lenny, he'll say whatever comes into his head. When I sat down in the chair opposite him in Dr. Phelan's waiting room, he asked me, "What's wrong with you?" At first I was going to snap back something like "None of your business," but when I saw his face, so shy and friendly, I couldn't help but tell him about my varicose veins. "I'm on my feet a lot," I said. Then he said, "I'm here to find out if I've got Agent Orange or just some dumb allergy," and he opened his top shirt buttons and showed me his red, raw chest. "Horrible, isn't it?" he said. "I look like a napalmed gook. Isn't that a joke?" I must have made a face because he said, "I'm sorry, I've got to learn to shut up. I've got a big mouth, and I don't think before I open it." Then he grinned and pointed at his head. "Post-traumatic Stress Disorder," he said, rolling his eyes. The way he said it made me laugh, but only for a second, and then I was embarrassed. I felt like I had to say something, so I said, "Have you been coming to Dr. Phelan long?" And he said, "You know, you're really pretty. But you shouldn't wear green. I think you'd look better in blue. A light blue, powder blue I think they call it. It'd show off that frosting in your hair."

It wasn't long before we started going out, and when he lost his job at Accurate Plastics and couldn't pay his rent, I took him in. I felt sorry for him, I guess, and maybe I even thought I was in love with him. I can't remember now. At any rate, he was only going to stay until he found a new job. But when he started working at the Remington plant, he asked if he could stay—just until he got back on his feet again—and I said yes. Then he lost that job too. For weeks, he looked for work, but then he started staying home, sitting in the La-Z-Boy and watching reruns of "The Honeymooners" and "I Love Lucy." All he did was sit there and smoke cigarettes and drink beer. When I came home, he'd tell me he'd been out looking for work, but I knew better. Once I picked up his ashtray and counted thirty-seven cigarette butts, then asked him if he expected me to believe he'd been out looking for jobs all day. That was when he first asked me to marry him. "I love you, Gloria," he said. "I won't ever be any good without you. If you just say yes, I'll be a new man. You'll see." He'd caught me off guard, and I didn't know what to say. I just stood there a moment, looking at him, trying to think of something I could tell him. Then he turned and walked over to the picture window and looked out at the rain. "To hell with Roy," he said. "When are you gonna forget about him? Do you think he lays awake nights thinking about *you*?" Then I said we shouldn't discuss such an important thing when we were tense and angry. "Let's talk about this tomorrow," I said. And the next morning, at breakfast, I told him I needed more time to think about it. After that, he asked me every day for a couple of weeks, and I always said I didn't know yet. After a while, he stopped asking, at least in words. But every time I came home I could see the question in his eyes.

I was crying as I drove home that night, thinking one minute how sad Lenny would be when I told him my answer and then the next how that man leaned over the table and kissed that girl, like no one else was in the restaurant or the world. When I pulled into the

BEAUTIFUL OHIO

driveway, I just sat there a minute, wiping mascara off my cheeks and trying to prepare myself. I didn't want to have to hurt Lenny, but even more I wanted everything settled; I wanted things simple, clear.

As soon as I opened the car door, I could hear that music again, and I knew Lenny was drunk. Whenever he drinks too much, he puts on Big Band music. It was the first thing he heard when he came home from Vietnam. As soon as he got his discharge at Fort Ord, he hitched a ride back to Little Rock with a buddy, and when he walked in the house, his mother was baking bread and listening to "Moonlight Serenade" on the hi-fi. She hadn't been expecting him for another week. After they hugged and kissed and cried, she gave him a slice of bread fresh from the oven and they sat in the kitchen and listened to Glenn Miller together. He'd never liked that kind of music before, but now he did, because sitting there, listening to those songs and eating that bread, he couldn't believe in the war anymore. It was just gone, a bad dream. He felt so happy he got up and danced right there in the kitchen with his mother, danced his idea of a waltz, both of them crying away.

I slammed the car door and started up the walk. Lenny was playing "In the Mood" so loud I knew he was in bad shape. Mrs. McDougal across the street had probably already called the police. I walked up the steps and put the key in the lock. Then I just stood there a moment, looking at the peeling siding Lenny had promised to scrape and paint, the broken shutters, the overgrown shrubs. Finally, I turned the key and stepped in. The living room was warm, all the lights on. I didn't see Lenny anywhere.

"Turn that thing down," I yelled.

Lenny came out of the kitchen then, wearing a blue apron that was dusty with flour. His hands were white too and he held them out in front of him, like Frankenstein in the movies.

"Gloria," he said. "You're home."

"Lenny," I said. "You're drunk."

He wiped his hands on a corner of the apron, then turned down the record player. "No, I'm not," he said. "I'm *plastered.*" Then he went back into the kitchen. After a second, I heard him kneading dough on the squeaky table. It was midnight, and he was baking bread. I set my purse on the endtable and sat down on the old flowered loveseat. For a second, I thought of just blurting it out: *I don't love you. I don't want to marry you.* But I decided to wait, to build up to it so he wouldn't take it so hard.

In a few minutes, Lenny came out of the kitchen, still wearing his apron, and sat down in the La-Z-Boy next to the loveseat. I could hear the timer ticking away in the kitchen. He always lets the bread rise three times, thirty minutes a time. That meant it'd be at least an hour, maybe two, before he was done baking. I saw him sitting in the La-Z-Boy, waiting to take his bread out of the oven, while I slept in the bedroom alone, and I suddenly felt so sorry for him I thought I'd wait until tomorrow to tell him. But I knew I couldn't. I couldn't wait even one more night.

Doris Day was singing "Sentimental Journey" now. "What music," Lenny said, nodding toward the record player. "You can just see all the people dancing. The whole country dancing." He looked at me, woozy, and blinked his eyelids hard. "I'm making bread," he said.

"I know," I answered, and tried to smile.

He looked away then and sighed. "I thought you'd never get home," he said. "The time, it's been moving so slow tonight."

I didn't say anything. Lenny sighed again, then tapped a Winston out of the pack on the endtable and lit it. Taking a long drag, he leaned his head back and exhaled slowly. Lately, his rash had started up his neck, and I wondered if one day it'd cover his face. I imagined his face raw and burned-looking, and I shivered.

Without looking at me, he said, "Hear anything interesting at work?"

For some time now, all we talked about was other people's conversations. It was easier than having our own. Sometimes, when I hadn't overheard anything interesting, I made something up, just to have something to talk about. But that night I didn't have to make anything up. I told him about the clay-eaters, just like I heard it, only I said it was two businessmen from Memphis who told me about them. Somehow, telling the story exhausted me. I wanted to go to bed and sleep.

"Clay?" he said, blowing out a stream of smoke. "Actual *clay*?"

"That's right. River clay. They dig it up right out of the banks of the Ohio."

Lenny threw his head back like a wolf and laughed. Then he began to sing. "Drifting with the current down a moonlit stream, While above the Heavens in their glory gleam . . ." He laughed again, softer this time. "The beautiful Ohio," he said, shaking his head. Then, his voice suddenly quiet, almost a whisper, he said, "Gloria, you're killing me. Don't you know that?"

I got up.

"Where are you going?" Lenny asked.

"I need a drink. I'll be right back."

Switching on the kitchen light, I saw the crockery bowl on the table, a dishtowel over it and, beside it, the timer, ticking hard and fast like my heart. I opened the cupboard where we kept the liquor and took down a bottle of Evan Williams and poured myself half a tumbler, then filled it with cold water from the tap. I took a couple of long swallows there at the sink, and felt my insides burn.

"Gloria," Lenny called.

"Just a minute," I yelled back. I took a long, deep drink, then started back out to tell him it was all over.

Lenny's head was slumped down over his chest and his eyes were closed, so for a second I thought he'd passed out and I could go to sleep in peace. But then he lifted his head and, eyes still closed, said, "Blue Moon." He pointed to the stereo. "People fell in love dancing to that song."

I had to say something, but I didn't know what. For weeks I'd been trying to decide what I'd say—I wanted it to be something gentle but firm, affectionate but cool—but I could never concentrate enough to get the words right. My mind always slipped ahead to the morning after, when I'd wake up alone and sit at the kitchen table drinking coffee and watching the sparrows play at the feeder outside the window. I saw myself sitting there, the room warm with sunlight, the birds making their quiet music, and I knew I wanted that moment more than anything.

I sat back on the loveseat and took another burning swallow of bourbon.

"Lenny," I finally said. But then I found I didn't have any other words.

"What?" Lenny turned to look at me. He was chewing on his mustache.

I took another drink. "Nothing," I said.

"No," he said. "You were going to say something."

"I've forgotten," I said. "It'll come to me later."

Lenny stood up then, swaying a little. He looked at me a moment, like he was about to say something, but he bit his lip and sat back down.

"Gloria," he whispered. "Tell me."

I looked down at my lap. Finally, I said, "I want to have a talk with you." It was a simple sentence, but after I said it, I was out of breath.

Lenny looked up at the ceiling and sighed. "I'd like us to have a baby," he said. "I want us to be a family. I want to do all the things families do. I want to push our baby down the aisles of Safeway in a shopping cart. Get Christmas cards made from a photograph. Sit in the barbershop while he gets his hair cut. And every year on his birthday draw a line on the doorjamb to show how much he's grown." He looked back at me. "After we die, there'll be nothing left of either of us."

That was the one way Lenny was like Roy—he wanted a baby too. I'd told him time and again that I was too old but he never listened. It wasn't that I didn't want a baby. I'd wanted to have one with Roy, but he had something wrong with him. His sperm count was okay, Dr. Phelan said, but for some reason they moved too slow. Dr. Phelan even removed a varicose vein from his testicle, figuring it was making his sperm too hot to move fast enough. But that didn't do anything either. Every now and then I wonder if he ever got that dropout pregnant. Sometimes I hope he did, and sometimes I don't.

I looked at Lenny, his sad face. "We talked about this before," I said.

Lenny stubbed out his cigarette in the ashtray. "No, we haven't. Not really. I've talked, but you haven't."

"What's that supposed to mean?"

Lenny looked at me. "Just what are you so scared of?"

I started to get up. "Maybe we should talk about this when you're not drunk."

"I'm not drunk," he said, taking my arm.

"Yes, you are."

"Okay, so I'm drunk. What's your excuse?"

"*Please*," I said, but I wasn't sure what I was begging for.

"Okay," Lenny said and let go of my arm. "Just sit down. I won't say anything more about a baby."

I sat down. The stereo was playing "Chattanooga Choo-Choo."

"Can we turn that thing off?" I said. "Can't we just sit here in quiet?"

Lenny got up and switched it off. Then he turned to face me. "I was hoping," he said, then closed his eyes and swallowed hard, "I

43

was hoping we'd do some dancing tonight. I was hoping this would be the night. I even bought some champagne and"—he gestured toward the kitchen—"I'm baking bread."

He looked so sad standing there that I closed my eyes, and for some reason I found myself thinking back to a day years ago when I was still in high school, long before I'd even met Roy. I was sitting in a dark classroom staring at the slides Mr. Moffett had taken that summer in Spain. There were castles on high cliffs, cathedrals, goatherds leading their flocks beside mountain roads, white houses with red tile roofs, markets full of tapestries, sheep's heads, fish, and pots, and dancers in red and black whirling under colored lights—so many amazing and beautiful things. I remembered imagining myself standing on a castle parapet, looking out over hills of olive trees, the wind whipping my hair off my forehead. Someday, I vowed, I'd go there. Even the names Mr. Moffett recited in the darkness made me ache to be there: Salamanca. Jaén. Torremolinos.

I opened my eyes and looked at Lenny. "I don't know what to say to you," I said. "I really don't."

"I'm going to get a job," Lenny said. "Really, I am. I've decided to go into refrigeration. Appliance work. I could take a couple of courses. There're lots of jobs. Small engine repair. Things are breaking down everywhere and I could fix them."

"It doesn't matter," I said. "That's not what I'm talking about."

"What are you talking about?"

I took another swallow of the bourbon. "Don't make me say it," I said.

"Okay," he answered. "Let's talk about something else. Let's talk about Roy and his little sweetheart, okay? What do you think they're doing right now?"

"Lenny," I said. "Stop."

"Do you think maybe they're dancing and drinking champagne and—"

"Please stop," I said.

"Stop what?" he said, swaying before me. "Breathing?"

"Don't you talk to me like that," I said, and shook my finger at him. Then I felt foolish, like a schoolteacher scolding a little child.

Lenny hung his head. "Gloria," he said. Just my name, nothing else.

"It's late," I started to say.

Lenny looked up then. His face was wet. "Don't leave me," he said.

The day Roy left, I was already late for work but I went into the kitchen where he was packing and reminded him to take some silverware or some of the beer glasses he liked. He was just piling things into a Jack Daniels box. I remember telling him he should wrap the glasses with some newspaper; that way they wouldn't break. And all the time I'd wanted to say, *Please don't go.*

I said yes. He held me against him, and I said, "Your apron . . . the flour," but he said, "It doesn't matter" and kissed me. Then he said, "Let's take the champagne to bed." I said, "But the bread . . ." and he said, "Let it keep rising."

In bed, he started to touch me. I wanted to say no, but I couldn't. I had already said yes. Such a simple word, almost a hiss. I wanted to say I was too tired, too . . . something, but I didn't dare, not now. I let him take my panties off, and I let him enter me bare, without a rubber, for the first time.

"I love you," he was saying, as he rocked on top of me. I thought about all those nights Roy and I tried to make a child, all those nights he came in me again and again. And I thought of the bread rising in the kitchen, rising over the lip of the crockery bowl, huge, and then Lenny kissed me and I tasted smoke and beer in his mustache and I thought *The smell of coffee and sunlight. The quiet music of the sparrows. Torremolinos.*

And suddenly I felt bloated, not with child, but with *clay*, and I

45

saw myself lying there, on the banks of the beautiful Ohio, my mouth and hands smeared with clay. I shut my eyes on that vision, and Lenny arched over me, holding himself at arms' length above me, and moved in me faster and faster until finally he came. "Oh," he said then, and it could have been a word in a foreign language: I didn't know what it meant, whether happiness or discovery or pain or surprise. And then he lowered his weight down on me.

The Bigs

I AM a baseball player. I come here from the Dominican Republic the home of Juan Marichal because baseball can't make you the same much of money in the Dominican League. That is why I live in the U S of A and play baseball for the Arkansas Travelers which are a team in the Texas League but live in Arkansas. The Arkansas Travelers are a team which is called a Double A team, meaning not so good as Triple A or Major Leagues—what everybody call The Bigs. Everybody here want to make it to The Bigs. There is no Bigs in the Dominican Republic and that is why I am living here so miserable and now that my family leave me I am more miserable ever than before. The only time I smile is after when I win a big game or if I forget for some minute and think my little Angelita is waiting at home for me to kiss her for goodnight. But tonight I am more miserable than I think a dead man because Coach he suspend me off the team and all because they leave me.

I love baseball. I love to pitch the ball. When I am the pitcher everybody depend of me, if I just stand there and hold the ball nobody do nothing. When I throw the ball everything happen. It is a good feeling but not the same as love which is something I have too much of I think. My heart it feel like it is in shreds each time when I think about Angelita and her black braids. And Pilar. I can not even say her name now without wanting to cry. Pilar is so beautiful, sometimes when I was in her I could not breathe right. When I think about her gone and Angelita with her I want to be on the mound throwing hard like Juan Marichal who come from Santo Domingo the same like me. I am a starter so I pitch the ball each four days, no more, and the rest of the time it go by so slow. I want I could pitch the ball each night if I will not tear my shoulder which is what I do at St. Peterburg my year of being a rookie when I try to show off I have stuff. Now my shoulder it hurt when I think about Pilar and Angelita so I try not to think about them when I am pitching the ball. But most of the time it is of no use because I think about them anyway. That is why I get in such big trouble tonight, I think of them when I should be thinking curve ball or slider, down or up.

The nights they are the most bad. I have dreams. Jackie say I grind my teeth when my dreams get so bad and when I wake up I am all wet with sweating and scared. Jackie try to make me all right then but it never work. She hug me and kiss me and say it only is a dream. Then I tell her what I dream and she say what it mean like a *curandera*. Some times I dream Pilar is opening her legs for Antonio who was sent back to Santo Domingo for weak field and no hit. Other times I dream I am pitching the ball when Angelita run out on the field with her arms reaching out for me but I don't see her before it is too late and I have already throw the ball and it hit her in the face and make her be dead. To me the dreams mean I love Pilar and Angelita so much my heart want to die. Twice I almost buy a gun and shoot my head. But Jackie say a gun is dumb, she say my dreams mean I should get married again and show Pilar some thing or two. She tell me to stop being a Mr. Sadface. That's what she call me when she try to make me smile. I know she want to marry with me by these signs but I don't want to marry with her, I want her to go away and leave me to be alone.

Pilar take Angelita back to the Dominican Republic because she don't care about The Bigs. She don't care about Juan Marichal or the Hall of Fame or driving a car with electric windows. She miss her mama and papa and the pacaya grove in her yard in Santo Domingo. When she look at the photographs of home that was when she would start crying and then a minute later yell at me for taking her to the U S of A. She don't understand English so good and no one except Antonio who play second base like a hole in his glove also speak Spanish. And she don't understand baseball too. To her it make no sense, to her it is crazy to pitch a ball that no one can hit it. She say to watch a game if no one hit the ball is no fun so I should make the batter to hit some home runs. She say Why you keep everybody from having fun, you think the fans pay so much of money to see pop-ups. She is a woman and she think like a woman. Still I did not suspect her to leave me. The trouble I am in tonight is all because she leave me. I try to tell Coach so he understand but still he suspend me off the team maybe for good. He have a wife who never leave and no kids.

The day Pilar go I pitch six and two-third no-score innings against the Shreveport Captains which are a team too in the Texas League, East Division. Then my arm it get sore and Coach say to get a shower and ice my shoulder up. I think now my shoulder ache because Pilar and Angelita are going that same minute. It was a sign but I don't see it then because I am wondering if Parisi will lose my win for me like usual, the rag arm. But this time he is lucky and I don't lose my win but because I am worrying so hard I miss the sign. God give all of us signs like a manager so we know what He want us to do. But now I don't know what to do. I don't see any signs. I think maybe God is mad with me and I am scared.

The night Pilar and Angelita leave I am halfway to almost

home when all of a sudden I know what my sore arm mean and I drive fast with my foot down on the floor and run through red lights one after each other and squeal into the parking lot like a madman. I go up the curb and almost into the swimming pool next by the apartment manager's office I am so much scared they have left me. And when I open the door Pilar and Angelita are gone and I can not find them everywhere. I look in the kitchen and living room and both bedrooms even behind the shower curtain but they are so gone I can feel how they are not there. I sit down on the bathroom floor and look at the shower curtain which Pilar buy when Angelita pull the other one down. She buy it because there is parrots on it like in our country and palm trees. I am so much sad I want to hold this curtain against me tight.

I did not think she would leave, I think only she talk about it. But now I see she mean what she say. After when I get up from the bathroom floor I go back in the kitchen and find what I did not see at first, a note sticked on the refrigerator door with a yellow smiling face magnet. It say in Spanish If you don't make The Bigs come to home and be a family again. I sit down then and put my big dumb head in my hands and cry. Mr. Sadface.

I don't know why I stayed in Little Rock. I should have went to Santo Domingo that same minute. Maybe there is something wrong with inside of me that make me stay. Maybe I don't love Pilar and Angelita like I think so. Maybe I want to hurt them like they do me. Or maybe I don't want to be like Antonio and go back to home the same I left, a worthless nothing. When I go back I want to be like Juan Marichal who is a Hall of Fame pitcher with more strikeouts than dogs in Santo Domingo. I want World Series rings on all my fingers and a car so big it have a TV in it and a bar. But I want more my Pilar and Angelita I think. Why I did not go back I am not sure but maybe I should have went before all this happen, before I become this disgrace to my country and my family. Before I have to go back with no choice of my own.

Jackie she think I stay because of her but that is not right. Jackie mean almost nothing to me. She was Willie Williams' girl last year and after he dump her still she come around and ask to go for a ride in his car which he call his Love Chariot. But he always say No and Get lost and one night I am so lonely I get mad and say Manny you don't have to take this shit off of Pilar that bitch you can have some fun too. So when Jackie come around at The Press Box to drink beers and shoot pool after we lose the doubleheader to Tulsa I say Willie that's no way to hurt a lady and make him say he is sorry so I don't hit him. After that she have her hands all over me. Now she stay here and sleep on Pilar's side of the bed but I want her to go because she is not Pilar. She wear a blonde wig and laugh like she is underneath angry. But she love me and go crazy with crying when I say some things like I don't want you to hang your wig on the doorknob. I can't say anything mad or she will cry and want to be dead so how can I tell her to get lost. She laugh a lot but she have a scar on both wrists from when Willie first tell her to go away. The scars look like X's cut so careful and neat, I can see her trying to make them pretty, her tongue sticking out the corner of her mouth while she do it, concentrating. I am scared she will kill herself dead so I make sex with her but I wish she would go away. She scare me with her crazy too much of love, like I scare myself.

Now I don't know what to do. Each day that pass I wait for a sign. But nothing happen. I want one minute to go home, I want that Pilar will lay on top of me and kiss me so I am lost in the dark cave of her so beautiful black hair. And I want to kiss Angelita for goodnight on her little nose and say to her like before the joke about the bed bugs biting. But another minute I want hard to be a baseball pitcher in The Bigs and hear everybody even the white people cheering my name. I want everybody to know I make the money they don't. I want a house with chandeliers and shag carpet everywhere and a swimming pool in the backyard with color lights under the water. I want all these things but I don't want Jackie with

51

her blonde wig and eye make-up and crying. But more than this I don't want her to bleed to death because I leave her like she always threaten without saying. So I want to go and I want to stay. And that make me not want anything anymore.

That is why I don't finish the game tonight. I am pitching the ball so good they swing and grunt at my curve ball which break in the dirt and my slider low and away. It is already inning eight and still I have no hits on me. Only six more outs to a no-hitter which would make Whitey Herzog to see I am ready for The Bigs. My palm it is sweating so I turn to pick up the bag of resin and then I see on the scoreboard all the zeros and somehow it take the breath out of me it all look so perfect. I am so proud because I do it, I make all the zeros. And then I think about Pilar leaving and Jackie's scars and my dream with Angelita running on the field and my pitch hitting her dead. Why I think these things then I do not know but I think them and it make my heart to beat so hard.

When I turn back to the plate my legs they are shaking like in my first game for los Azucareros del Este when Pilar was in the stands to cheer for me and I imagine she is out there now watching me and knowing if I do good I will make The Bigs and marry with Jackie because I am scared to find her in my bathtub, the water turning red. So I look down at Gene my catcher and nod and then I throw the ball and it sail over everybody's head and up the screen, a wild pitch. Gene he signal time and run out to the mound and say Jesus Christ Manny I give you the sign for change-up not fastball what are you thinking of. I can not remember what I say but Gene he go back to behind the plate and thump his mitt and give me another sign. I nod and throw the ball and it hit the batter in the shoulder and he spin around like he want to fight but I stand there only and look at him. Then he go down to first holding his shoulder and swearing at me and Gene he say Don't worry about it kid. You'll get 'em, he say. Just take it easy.

All this time I am thinking If I throw a no-hitter I will never see my Pilar and Angelita again. Not forever. So when Gene throw the ball back to me I am not watching close and it hit the top of my glove and don't go in. I look around quick and it isn't there. Gene he jump up then and yell Second! Second! but by the time when I find the ball and turn around to throw it to Peachy, already the runner he is standing up and brushing the dirt off his uniform. I hear Coach swear loud but somehow I don't care like I should.

Settle down, Gene say then and give me a sign. I start to wind up but then I forget what pitch he ask for and I stop, a balk. The runner he walk down to third laughing. I don't look at him. Gene come out to the mound then. Calm down for Chrissakes, Gene say. If they get a hit they get a hit the main thing is win. So just rare back and hump that ball in there. Okay I say and he go back. Then he give me a sign maybe for fastball or could be slider. But I just stand there and hold the ball. He give me another sign I think for curve but I just stand there. Then Gene come out to the mound again and Coach too this time and Coach he say What's the problem Manny your arm getting sore again. I shake my head no. Then what gives, he say. What the fuck is going on. I almost can not talk the words are so far down inside of me but somehow I say Nothing but I say it in Spanish—*Nada*. I never talk on the team in Spanish because in The Bigs they want that you always talk American. But I say *Nada*. Then he look at me foreign and ask You all right. I say Fine in American and he say Good let's set 'em down, then he trot back to the dugout and Gene go behind the plate and give me one more time again the sign and this time too I do nothing. If I do nothing nothing happen because I am the pitcher, I am the one who hold the ball. I want then everything to stop, I want time to stop, I want Jackie to stop, I want being alone and sad to stop, so I hold the ball for one minute. For that one minute the world stand still, nothing change, and I can breathe.

Then the umpire step before the plate and say Throw the ball Sanchez or it is delay of the game. The batter he step out of the box and shrug his shoulders to the dugout of his team and spit. I stand there more. Then Gene say What the fuck and everybody in the stands start to yell and boo but I don't do anything.

Then out of the dugout come Coach's face looking red. All of a sudden I feel so sorry for him, so sorry for Gene and Peachy and my teammates and for Jackie and Pilar and Angelita and the umpire and the people in the stands who are booing so disappointed. I feel so bad for everybody I want to cry. Then Coach he say What the hell do you think you're doing Sanchez. I say it again—*Nada*. And he say Don't give me any of that I want to know why you aren't throwing the goddamn ball. His face is close to mine the way he get with a umpire who make a lousy call. I look down and say from somewhere My wife she leave me and my little girl is gone away. Jesus H. Christ he say then and touch his left arm which mean bring in the lefty. Then he say You're under suspension Sanchez now get your sorry ass out of this park and don't come back until your head is on straight. I don't want to see you or hear you or even *smell* you until then is that clear. I just stand there and listen to him, I can't even nod. Everything I live for is disappearing into nothing, I am becoming like a zero, and I am sad but somehow all of a sudden I am so much of nothing I am gone away and I'm there but not there too and where I am is so peaceful I want almost to cry. I want to tell Coach about this place, I want to tell everyone, but there are no words there so I only smile at him. He look away then mad and cursing but still I smile so happy.

And I am still smiling when Parisi come in to take from me my no-hitter and make me a nobody who can not go to home or stay where he is without shame. I am holding the ball and everything have stop and I am so happy and I love everybody even Coach and the fans booing and Whitey Herzog who keep me from being in The Bigs so long and Antonio who steal my wife maybe. I love everybody so much I feel like I am dead and looking down on everybody from heaven, not a man anymore but a angel with no sadness or pain or anything, just love. But then Coach take the ball away from me and give it to Parisi. He take the ball away, he take everything away, and I am standing there waiting and alone and there is no sign.

Firelight

JIMMY hadn't planned to break the windows; he hadn't thought about it at all. He'd just been walking around the neighborhood, as he always did on the Saturdays his mother's boyfriend came to town. He'd left the apartment so quickly that he'd forgotten his mittens, and he walked with his hands balled in his jacket pockets. He thought about going back to get his mittens, but once when he'd gone home before he was supposed to, his mother and her boyfriend were in her bedroom with the door closed, making noises. He knew what those noises meant because one day at recess a third-grader named Evan was talking about what grown-ups do in bedrooms. "It's the same as dogs," he'd said. Jimmy couldn't imagine his mother doing such a thing with anybody, especially that vacuum salesman from St. Paul with his thick glasses and hairy ears. And maybe she didn't do it after all. Maybe they were in her bedroom because she was too tired to sit up in the living room and talk. She was always tired, even though she didn't work at the cafe anymore, and she spent most days in bed anyway. But what were the noises then?

He tried to think of something else. He thought about the Teenage Mutant Ninja Turtles and the frog his friend Greg brought to school in a jar once and let loose in the lunchroom. Michael Jackson kept a brain in a jar in his bedroom, and Greg said that proved he was crazy. But Jimmy thought he probably just wished he could put that person's brain in his head, and that didn't seem crazy to him. But maybe that was because he was crazy, too. If he had Greg's brain, he'd know if he was or not. He imagined lying in bed, with Greg's brain in his head and his own brain in a jar on the dresser, and wondered what he'd think. But he couldn't guess. If his brain was normal, shouldn't he be able to guess what someone else would think?

His mother's brain definitely wasn't normal. Ever since his father left them, she'd had to take pills for her mind. Jimmy used to blame the way she was on his father, but maybe she wasn't much different before he left. His father used to call her a crazy bitch, so maybe that was why he left, because she was crazy even then. Jimmy didn't know. He couldn't remember much about that time, because he was so little. He barely even remembered his father. He just remembered that he was tall and had a mustache and smoked brown cigarettes. And he remembered how his big hands would hurt him when he picked him up under his arms, and how he liked him to pick him up anyway. Jimmy wondered where his father was now and what he was doing. His mother said he lived in Nebraska with his new family, and Jimmy wondered if Nebraska was a town or a state and how far away it was. And did his father ever pick up his new son the way he used to pick him up?

He was tired of walking around, so he decided to go over to the school playground. Kids were always there on weekends, playing on the swings and monkey bars or tossing a football back and forth. But when he got to the playground, no one was there. Even the houses across the street looked deserted. Everywhere he looked, there was nothing. Not even a stray dog. And suddenly he felt all alone. A long shiver snaked up his spine, and he wanted to go home and sit on the edge of his mother's bed and talk to her. But it wasn't six o'clock yet. Her boyfriend would still be there.

Nevertheless, he started walking slowly toward home, kicking rocks as he crossed the gravel playground. But when he'd rounded the south wing of the school, he stopped. The sun was setting in the long row of windows, making them glow with a beautiful, cold fire. He'd seen those windows many times before, but only today did he realize how easy it would be to break one. All you had to do was pick up a rock and throw it. Anybody could do it, but nobody ever did. Maybe you had to be crazy to do it. He picked up a rock, to see if he would throw it. What would Greg think if he saw him now? Would he try to talk him out of it? And what about his mother and his father? What would they say? Jimmy imagined his father walking down the sidewalk and seeing him with the rock in his hand. "Hey, Jimmy," he'd say. "Is that you?"

Then one of the windows exploded, and Jimmy jumped back, startled, and looked at his empty hand. He couldn't remember throwing the rock, but he had. And now that he'd done it, he felt so good, so suddenly *happy*, that he kept on picking up rocks and throwing them, breaking window after window, until he heard a car coming down the street and had to run away.

By Monday morning, when Jimmy went back to school, the janitors had swept up the glass and taped cardboard over the eighteen broken windows. After the bell rang, all the kids in his class were still standing by the windows, talking excitedly about who could have done it, and they didn't take their seats until Mrs. Anthony threatened to keep them inside during recess. And even before the class could recite the Pledge of Allegiance, the principal's voice came over the loudspeaker and said the guilty party would eventually be caught so he might as well turn himself in now. *The guilty party*—that was Jimmy. He tried not to look guilty, but the more he tried, the more he felt everyone knew he had done it. Ever since he'd broken the windows, he'd felt like a stranger in his own life, someone just pretending to be who he was, and he was sure everyone would see the change in his face if they looked. He stared at his desk intently, as if merely to look up would be a confession.

Later that morning, as the class was on its way out for recess, Mrs. Anthony stopped him at the door and asked if she could talk to him for a minute. He was sure, then, that she had found out, but when the others were gone, she only asked if he was feeling all right. "Have things been bad at home?" she said, her forehead furrowed and her husky voice soft. He knew she was talking about his mother—Mrs. McClure, the social worker, had told him she'd "explained everything" to Mrs. Anthony, so he could feel free to talk to her if anything was troubling him. "Yes," he lied, and the word seemed to take his breath away. "My mother was mean to me." And then he ran outside and sat under a maple tree near the swings, trying to get his breath back. Greg came over then and challenged him to a game of tetherball, but Jimmy said he didn't want to play. "Why not?" Greg said. "You chicken?" And even though Greg started to flap his arms and cluck like a chicken, Jimmy did not get up and chase him.

School ended that day without anyone accusing him of breaking the windows, but he was still certain he'd be caught. Maybe somebody already knew, but they hadn't said anything because they were testing him, trying to see if he would confess on his own. He didn't know what to think. It was like he had to learn a whole new way of thinking, now that he'd broken the windows. As he walked home, he tried out different things to say when he was accused. He could say it was all an accident—he'd been trying to hit some blackbirds that were flying past or something—or maybe

59

there was a robber, somebody breaking into the school, and he'd chased him away by throwing rocks at him and some of them hit the windows. But nothing he thought of sounded good enough, and after a while he gave up and tried to think of something else.

Though the afternoon was bright and sunny, the temperature had dropped below freezing. He hunched his shoulders against the cold and started down the street to the run-down clapboard house where he and his mother rented an apartment on the second floor. He was hoping his mother wasn't too tired to make hot chocolate for him. But then he saw the social worker's yellow Subaru parked in front of the house again and knew he wouldn't get any hot chocolate—or even any supper. After Mrs. McClure's visits, his mother was always so exhausted she'd have to go to bed for the rest of the day, and he'd have to make his own supper, and hers too. And that meant he'd have to eat hot dogs or toast again because they were the only things he could cook. And he'd have to watch TV by himself all night, too, and every now and then he'd probably hear her crying in her room. He knew better than to go in and try to comfort her, though; that only made her cry harder or, sometimes, yell at him.

He didn't want to go inside while Mrs. McClure was there, but it was so cold he went in the dark, musty entryway of the old house and climbed the steps up to the second-floor landing. Outside their apartment he hesitated a moment, then opened the door quietly. He hoped he could sneak through the kitchen and down the hall to his room without Mrs. McClure seeing him. Carefully he set his bookbag on the rug and hung his jacket on the coatrack. Then he heard his mother's voice coming from the living room.

"So I had a glass with lunch. I don't know what's the big hairy deal. Who appointed you my savior anyway?"

"Now, Marjorie, I don't think of myself as—"

"Look, why don't you just get the hell out of here. I'm sick to death of your stupid face. Just get out and leave me alone."

During the silence that followed, Jimmy's jacket suddenly slipped off the coatrack and landed with a muffled thud on the floor. "Jimmy?" his mother said. "Is that you?"

Jimmy sighed. "Yes," he said, and stepped to the doorway of the living room. Mrs. McClure turned in her chair. "Why hello, Jimmy! Aren't you getting to be a big boy?" She said things like that every time she saw him, as if she hadn't seen him just the week before. He hated that, and hated even more the times she tried to act like she was his mother. Last month, when it was time for parent-teacher conferences, she'd gone to his school and talked to Mrs. Anthony about the U he got in Conduct. She had no right to do that; that was his mother's job, not hers.

"Aren't you going to say hello, Jimmy?" Mrs. McClure said.

"Hi," Jimmy answered. But that didn't satisfy her; she kept looking at him, as if she were waiting for him to say something else, and he thought again how her long nose and chin made her look like a witch.

"Come on in and sit down," she said then, as if it were *her* apartment, but Jimmy stayed in the doorway. Finally, she turned back to his mother, who was lying on the couch in her flannel nightgown and blue terrycloth bathrobe, an arm crooked over her eyes to block out the light slanting through the tall windows. Mrs. McClure always opened the drapes when she came. "No wonder you're down in the dumps," she'd say. "You keep this place too dark." Now she said, "I suppose I should be going. But don't forget what I said about a new hairdo. I think you'd be surprised how much better you'd feel about yourself." She nodded her bangs at his mother's greasy brown hair to emphasize her point. "And the Rosary Society at St. Jacob's is sponsoring a clothing drive. Perhaps you'd like me to bring around a few things in your size?" Jimmy looked at Mrs. McClure and tried to imagine his mother wearing her pink dress and nylons, her hoop earrings and silver and turquoise bracelets. But he couldn't and he started to giggle. He didn't think it was funny, but he started to giggle anyway.

"Shush," his mother said, without removing her arm from her eyes. Some days, that was the only thing she said to him. She got headaches easily, so he had to be quiet around her. Sometimes he even watched TV with the sound off, guessing at what people were saying. It was kind of fun, watching the mouths move and no sounds come out, and sometimes in school he'd pretend he was deaf and dumb until Mrs. Anthony threatened to send him to the principal's office. Just thinking about how red Mrs. Anthony's face got when she was mad made him giggle more. He wished he could have seen her face when she first saw all the broken windows. He imagined it getting so red that steam blew out her ears, just like in the cartoons, and he started laughing. His mother gritted her teeth. "I said, *Stop it*." But he couldn't stop.

Mrs. McClure turned to look at him, her head tilted a little, like a bird listening for worms underground, and he began laughing hard. But then—he didn't know how it happened—he was crying. His mother didn't get up, but she pointed at him. "Now look what you've done," she said to Mrs. McClure.

"Look what *I've* done?" Mrs. McClure said. "Can't you see why he's crying? He's just come home from school and you haven't even said hello to him. All you've done is snap at him."

"Why don't you just shut the fuck up."

"I have a job to do, Marjorie, and I intend to do it. But if you're not interested in helping yourself, how can I possibly help you?"

His mother sat up slowly and leaned toward Mrs. McClure. "You can help me by getting the hell out of my apartment."

"Marjorie, you know that—"

"I said, *Get out*."

Mrs. McClure sighed and shook her head, then she turned to

Jimmy. "Don't cry, honey," she said. "Everything's going to work out in the end." She held out her arms. "Come here, sweetie."

For a second, he saw himself sitting in her lap, her arms around him, and he almost started toward her. That fact surprised him so much he stopped crying.

Mrs. McClure dropped her arms and sat there a moment, looking at him, then she slowly stood up. "Maybe I've done all I can do here," she said to his mother. "Maybe it's time to take your case to another level."

His mother glared at her. "Just what is that supposed to mean?" she asked. But Mrs. McClure only shook her head, then gathered up her manila folder and purse and started toward the door.

"You and your damned threats," his mother said to her back. "You can just go to hell."

Mrs. McClure didn't answer. She merely stopped for a second to tousle Jimmy's curly black hair and say, "Don't worry, we'll take care of you." Then she went out the door and down the steps.

"A new hairdo," his mother said then. "She can just go fuck herself." Jimmy looked at her. Normally her round face was pale and her eyes looked wet, as if she had just finished crying or was about to start, but now her skin was splotchy and her eyes looked fierce. "What are you staring at?" she said.

Jimmy wanted to ask what Mrs. McClure meant by "another level," but he didn't dare. "Do you want me to make you supper tonight?" Jimmy asked. "I can make hot dogs if we got some."

"Just shut the damned drapes," she said. "Shut all the god-damned drapes and leave me alone. I'm tired and I want to sleep." She lay back on the sagging couch and hugged herself. "And get me a blanket. It's cold in here."

"Okay," Jimmy said, and went around the room, closing the drapes. Then he got a spare blanket from the linen closet and started to cover his mother with it. Her eyes were closed and he thought she was already asleep, but she opened them and said,

"You're a good boy, Jimmy. I'm not mad at *you*. You know that, don't you?" When he nodded, she gave him the smile he loved so, the one that made her eyes crinkle up. "It's you and me," she said. "You and me against the world." And then she closed her eyes again and turned toward the back of the couch.

For the next two weeks, no one mentioned the windows, and Jimmy began to believe that he wouldn't be caught after all. Then one day he came home from school and heard his mother talking on the phone in the kitchen. "Think about Jimmy," she was saying, her voice wavering. "He doesn't deserve this." Then she was silent a long time before she said, "I'll be there. Just give me a chance to explain." When she hung up, he went into the kitchen. His legs felt funny, as if his knees had turned to water. He was sure she'd been talking to the principal, or maybe a policeman.

"Oh, you're home," she said, and wiped her nose with a Kleenex.

He was about to tell her it wasn't true, someone else broke the windows, when she suddenly said, "Look at this mess!" She gestured at the dirty dishes piled on the table and counters. "We've got to clean up everything right away." Then she began to fill the sink with water, but before it was even half full, she abruptly turned off the faucet. "We'd better do the bedrooms first," she said, and hurried to her room, where she started picking up clothes and newspapers and empty wine jugs from the floor. "Just look at all of this!" she said. She carried the load out into the living room and dumped it on the sofa. Then she straightened the sofa pillows and wiped dust off the coffee table with her palm. "Don't just stand there," she said then. "Help me clean up this mess!"

"What should I do?"

"You can do the dishes while I do the laundry." She led him back into the kitchen. "First," she said. But then she closed her eyes and shook her head slowly back and forth. "Oh, God, why did they have to come today? Just a half gallon of milk and a jar of jelly in the fridge. And me still in bed . . ." Then she looked at Jimmy. Her eyes were red and swollen, and he could smell the wine on her breath. "Damn it," she said. "Who the hell do they think they are?"

Jimmy realized then that the principal and the policeman must have come to the apartment looking for him. That frightened him, but he was relieved that his mother seemed madder at them than at him. She must not believe that he broke the windows. Maybe she thought he was too normal to do it, and maybe that meant he really was normal. She was his mother and she would know, wouldn't she? "What's wrong?" he finally dared to say.

"Nothing," she answered. "Nothing for you to worry about." Then she said, "To hell with the dishes. We'll do them tomorrow." And she went to bed and stayed there the rest of the night. Every now and then, Jimmy heard her crying, and then she'd begin cursing. Finally, she fell asleep, and Jimmy lay in his bed across the hall, listening to her peaceful breathing and wishing he could dream whatever she was dreaming, so he'd know what could make her happy.

The next morning, his mother surprised him by coming into the kitchen in a lacy lavender dress with puffy sleeves. Her hair was combed, and she had put on lipstick and rouge. She frowned and said, "Do I look all right?"

"You look pretty," Jimmy said, and took a bite of his toast.

"But do I look like a good mommy?" she asked. "Do I look like I clean my house and go to church and love you more than anything in the world?"

He started to smile, thinking she was teasing him, but the frightened look on her face made him stop. He looked down at his plate.

"I think so," he said.

All that week and most of the next, his mother dressed up each morning and left the apartment. She was looking for a new job, she told him, but every afternoon, when he came home from school and asked her if she'd found one, she said no. "But I'll keep trying," she said one day, then knelt down and hugged him tightly. "I won't give up. No matter how hard I have to fight, I won't give up."

But eventually she stopped dressing in the morning and started staying in bed all day, drinking wine, just as she had before. When Jimmy asked her why she wasn't looking for jobs anymore, she said, "What are you talking about?" Then she said, "Oh, that. Forget about that. There aren't any jobs for bad mommies, not a single one."

Then one morning Mrs. McClure came to the apartment for the first time in weeks. It took Jimmy a few minutes to realize she had come to take him away. "You're going to live somewhere else for just a little while," his mother said, her voice quivering. "It's all for your own good." Then she took his small face in her hands and kissed him goodbye. "Remember I love you," she said, and her mouth twisted as if the words made it hurt. "Now go." Then Mrs. McClure took his hand and led him outside to her car.

It was several months before Jimmy was to learn he had not been taken away from his mother because of the windows. That morning, though, he believed they had finally proved he'd done it and, because he was too young to go to jail, they were punishing him by sending him to some strangers' house, where they would watch him to make sure he didn't break any more windows. As he rode away from his home, he thought of telling Mrs. McClure he was innocent, but he was sure a teacher or janitor had seen him. And he knew that none of the excuses he had made up would work. So he didn't say anything; he just sat there, looking straight ahead while Mrs. McClure went on and on about Mr. and Mrs. Kahlstrom and how they had fixed up their spare room just for him. "They've painted the walls sea blue and they've put a huge toybox at the foot of the bed and filled it with Transformers and Lincoln Logs and everything else you can think of," she said. "How does that sound?" When he didn't answer, she said, "You don't have anything to worry about, Jimmy. Everything's going to be just fine. You know that, don't you?" Jimmy nodded, so she'd leave him alone. "That's good," she said then. "I'm glad you're being such a big brave boy."

But at the Kahlstroms' house, he wasn't brave for long. Standing in the entryway, Mrs. McClure cheerfully introduced him to the strangers who would be his temporary parents. Mrs. Kahlstrom was a small, bird-boned woman, and even though the house was warm and she was wearing a bulky turtleneck sweater, she kept hugging herself as if she were cold. She said, "Hello, Jimmy," and smiled so big he could see her gums. Mr. Kahlstrom shook his hand when he said hello. He was tall and thin and had an Adam's apple like Ichabod Crane in the story Mrs. Anthony had read to Jimmy's class. Jimmy was so scared he wanted to turn and run out the door, but his legs were trembling too much. He didn't know what to do, and he surprised himself as much as the others when he suddenly lay down on the rug and curled up like a dog going to sleep. The three adults hovered over him, startled looks on their faces. From the floor they looked so different it was almost as if they weren't people at all but some strange creatures from another world. Mrs. McClure took his elbow and asked him to please stand up like a good boy, but he jerked his arm away. They all tried to talk him into getting up, but he stayed on the floor, even when Mr. and Mrs. Kahlstrom tried to tempt him into the house by showing him some of the toys they'd bought. Finally Mrs. McClure said it might be best just to let him lie there until he was ready to get up. "I don't know what to say," she told the Kahlstroms. "I've never seen a reaction like this." Mrs. Kahlstrom offered him a sofa pillow then, but he shook his head, so she just set it on the linoleum beside him. Then Mrs. McClure shook their hands and said goodbye, and Mr. and Mrs. Kahlstrom went into the living room to wait for Jimmy to get up and join them.

For a time after Mrs. McClure left, Jimmy could hear them whispering. Then he heard a sudden sharp sob, and Mr. Kahlstrom saying, "There, there, dear. Just give him time." Then they went into another room, farther away, and he couldn't hear them anymore. After a while, a phone rang somewhere, and Jimmy heard Mr. Kahlstrom answer it, then say, "No, not yet" and "We'll let you know as soon as anything happens" and "Thanks for calling." A long time later, Mr. Kahlstrom came, squatted down on his haunches, and set a plate beside the rug. "It's lunchtime, Jimmy," he said. "Mrs. McClure told us you liked Sloppy Joes and potato chips. I hope that's right." When Jimmy didn't say anything, he let out a long sigh, then stood up and went away. Jimmy was hungry, but he wasn't going to eat anything until they took him back home. He'd starve himself, and if that didn't work, he'd just break all the windows in the house. And if Mrs. McClure took him somewhere else, he'd break all the windows there, too; he'd break all the windows everywhere, until she'd finally have to take him back to his mother again.

A half-hour later, when Mr. Kahlstrom returned, Jimmy still hadn't eaten anything, but he was sitting up now and crying. "I'm sorry," he said. "I won't break any of your windows, I promise. Just let me go home, please. Please let me go home."

Mr. Kahlstrom knelt down beside Jimmy. "Sorry? You don't have anything to be sorry about. And you don't have to worry about breaking any of our windows, or anything else either. Just feel free to play and do everything you do in your own house. And if something does break, don't worry about it—we can get it fixed. All right?"

Jimmy looked at him. Maybe he didn't know about the windows, maybe Mrs. McClure didn't tell either of them. "All right," he said.

"Say," Mr. Kahlstrom said then, "I bet your Sloppy Joe is cold.

What do you say we head into the kitchen and make you another one?"

For the next two months, whenever Mrs. McClure asked, Jimmy told her that he liked living with the Kahlstroms. And mostly, he did. Mr. Kahlstrom taught music at the high school, and he played songs for Jimmy on the big upright piano in the living room. Jimmy's favorite was one called "Down at Papa Joe's." Mr. Kahlstrom showed Jimmy how to play the melody—he took his small hand with his big one and helped him poke out the notes with one finger—and Jimmy liked that. But he didn't like it when Mrs. Kahlstrom sat down on the corner of the piano bench beside them. She had scared him his third night there, when she tucked him into bed, by telling him that she and Roger—that was what she called Mr. Kahlstrom—had once had a little boy very much like him but that he had swallowed some gasoline and died when he was only three. It had been eleven years since he died and they still missed him, and that was why they had decided to become foster parents. She reached out her bony hand when she said that and brushed the hair away from his forehead. "He had curly hair too," she said, "only his was blond."

The Kahlstroms were nice to him. Mr. Kahlstrom took him up to the high school on weekends and let him play with all the different drums in the band room, and he bought him a Nerf football so they could play Goal Line Stand in the living room. Mrs. Kahlstrom worried about the furniture and lamps, but she let them play anyway, and when Jimmy tackled Mr. Kahlstrom she'd clap and say, "Way to go, Jimmy!" Mrs. Kahlstrom made him bacon and eggs for breakfast nearly every day and helped him with his home-work and took him to the matinee on Saturdays, but she was so nervous all the time that she made him nervous too. And she was always talking about love. She had loved him even before she met

him, she said. And at night, after she read him a story, she'd kiss
him on his nose just like he was a little kid still and say she loved,
loved, loved him so much she could eat him up. Then she'd sit
there a moment, as if she were waiting for him to say "I love you"
back, before she'd finally get up and turn out the lights. And the
stories she read bothered him too. They were stupid stories, little
kid stories. Once she read one about a dog that was on the ark with
Noah. The dog seemed to think the flood came along just so he
could have a good time, sailing around and playing games with the
other animals. He never even thought about all the dogs that got
drowned. His own parents had probably drowned in the flood, and
his brothers and sisters too. But he didn't seem to care. And when
the flood was over and Noah picked him for his pet, he jumped up
and down like he was the luckiest dog in history.

Each Friday, Mrs. McClure came to visit for a few minutes. She
never mentioned the windows, but Jimmy knew she hadn't forgotten about them, because she always told him he couldn't go home
just yet. He wished she'd tell him how long he was going to be
punished, but all she'd ever say was, "It won't be much longer now,
sweetheart." At first he thought he'd have to stay at the Kahlstroms'
for eighteen days—one for each window—but when the eighteenth
day came and went without her coming to take him home, he
began to worry it'd be eighteen weeks. But then, a few days before
Christmas, she called and told him to pack his things because she
was coming to take him home. At the door, Mr. Kahlstrom shook
his hand and hugged him. "Be good, Jimmy," he said, patting his
back. Mrs. Kahlstrom wasn't there; she was upstairs in her room,
and although he couldn't hear her, Jimmy knew she was crying.
"Tell Mrs. Kahlstrom . . ." he said, but he didn't know what he
wanted him to tell her, so he stopped. Then Mrs. McClure took his
hand and led him down the sidewalk to her car. He wanted to turn
around and see if Mrs. Kahlstrom was watching from her window
upstairs, but he didn't.

On the way home, Mrs. McClure mentioned that his mother had been at a hospital in St. Paul. "What was she doing there?" he asked.

"Getting better," Mrs. McClure answered. "Wait till you see her. She's a new person now."

And she was, too, at least for a while. His first day back, she told him he was the best Christmas present she had ever gotten, and she baked a turkey and made mashed potatoes and gravy. And afterward, she gave him a present—"Just one, for now," she said, "You'll have to wait till Christmas Eve for the rest." It was a Nerf football, just like the one Mr. Kahlstrom had bought for him. He looked at her. Her chin was trembling. "Mrs. McClure told me you liked playing football," she said. "I thought maybe we could play a little sometime."

They only played a couple of times, though, before she started getting tired again. The first Saturday after Christmas she went to bed right after breakfast. Jimmy watched cartoons in the living room all morning, then made himself a peanut butter and jelly sandwich for lunch. After he finished it, he went into her room to ask her if she wanted something to eat, too. She was standing in front of her bureau mirror. She was still in her nightgown, but she was wearing a strange white hat with a pink ribbon around its brim. Jimmy wasn't sure, but he thought he'd seen that hat before. Then he remembered: it was her Easter hat, and she'd worn it back when his father lived with them and they still went to church. "Are you going to church, Mom?" he asked. She turned around, and he saw that she'd been crying. For a moment, he was worried that she was going to say something about the windows. But then she said, "While I was in the hospital, I got a letter from Mr. Gilchrist. You remember Mr. Gilchrist, don't you?" Jimmy nodded. Mr. Gilchrist was the vacuum salesman who made the noises with her in the bedroom. "Well, he said he wouldn't be coming to town anymore. He said his company changed his route." She laughed abruptly, then frowned. "Men," she said. She looked at him. "I wish you weren't a boy, Jimmy. You'll grow up to be just like the rest of them, and you'll leave me too."

"No I won't," Jimmy said.

"Yes you will."

"No I won't," he repeated, shaking his head.

"Goddamn it, you *will*," she said, and tore the hat off her head and flung it against the wall. Jimmy flinched and took a step backward. "I'm sorry," she said then. "I didn't mean it." She reached out for him. "Come here, honey. I'm sorry."

But he didn't move.

"All right then," she said, and dropped her hands to her sides. "Do whatever the hell you want. You will anyway." She got back into bed and pulled the covers up to her chin. Jimmy stood there, watching her. "What are you waiting for?" she said. "*Go.*" And he left.

The next day she was better—she even helped him build a snow fort in the yard until she got too tired—and Jimmy thought everything was going to be all right again. But by mid-January, she was so tired all the time that she had to go back to the hospital. Mrs. McClure said she was a lot better than she had been, but she still wasn't quite well. When Jimmy asked what was wrong with her, she said, "It's nothing to worry about. She just needs a rest." Jimmy tried to convince her that his mother could rest at home— he could clean the house for her and do the laundry and cook—but she only sighed. "It's not just for a rest, Jimmy. Your mother's not very happy right now. At the hospital they'll help her be happy again."

Jimmy didn't say anything then. He knew why she was unhappy; it was all his fault. Why had he thrown those rocks? If he had just put that first rock down and walked away, she wouldn't have to go back to the hospital and he wouldn't have to go back to the Kahlstroms'. He didn't want to live there anymore. It wasn't that he didn't like the Kahlstroms—he did—but he missed his mother when he was there. Most people didn't know how nice she was; they only saw her when she was too tired to be nice. But sometimes when he'd tell her something funny that happened at school she'd laugh so hard she'd have to hold her sides and smile so big there'd be wrinkles around her eyes. He loved that smile, and in the weeks that followed, he often stood in front of the Kahlstroms' bathroom mirror and tried to imitate it. He'd stand there for a long time, smiling at himself with her smile, until Mrs. Kahlstrom would get worried and come looking for him.

This time, his mother got out of the hospital after only a month, but Mrs. McClure said he couldn't go home just yet. He cried so hard then that the Kahlstroms agreed to let his mother come once a week for a visit. That Sunday, Mrs. McClure dropped her off in her Subaru. Jimmy was upstairs in his room when the doorbell rang. "Your mother's here," Mr. Kahlstrom called, and Jimmy came running downstairs just as he opened the door for her. It was snowing lightly and her hair and the shoulders of her coat were dusted with snow. "Come on in, Mrs. Holloway," he said, and helped her out of her coat. "Welcome to our home."

She didn't look at him. She just cleared her throat and said, "Thank you," then looked at Jimmy, who was standing beside the potted fern in the hall. "Jimmy," she said, and knelt on one knee for him to come to her. He had been looking forward to her coming, but now that she was here, he felt strangely shy, and he walked toward her slowly, with his eyes down. Then her arms were around him and she was kissing his cheek. She didn't smell like herself, though; she was wearing perfume that smelled like the potpourri Mrs. Kahlstrom kept in an Oriental dish in the bathroom. He stepped back and looked at her. Her eyebrows looked darker and there were red smudges on her cheekbones. As she stood up, her silver earrings swung back and forth. She was smiling, but it wasn't her real smile, the one she gave him when they were alone.

"If you'd like, you can sit in the living room," Mr. Kahlstrom said. "I've just built a fire in the fireplace." He led them to the living room. "I'll leave you two alone," he said then, and went upstairs to join Mrs. Kahlstrom, who had told Jimmy at breakfast that she hoped he'd understand but she just couldn't be there when his mother came.

Jimmy sat in the wingback chair beside the white brick fireplace and swung his legs back and forth. His mother stood in front of the fire a moment, warming herself and looking at Mrs. Kahlstrom's collection of Hummel figurines on the mantel, then sat down on the end of the sofa next to the chair. He knew he should go sit with her, but he didn't. Then she touched the cushion beside her and said, "Won't you come sit with me?" He nodded and slid out of the chair and climbed up next to her. It felt strange to be alone with his mother in someone else's house—it was like they were actors in a movie or something and not real people. He didn't know what to say to her. He wasn't at all tired, but he stretched and yawned. He didn't know why he'd done that, and he suddenly wanted to be upstairs in his room, playing with his toys, the visit over and his mother on her way back home.

"Mr. Kahlstrom made a fire," he finally said, though she already knew that. Then he added, "He showed me how to do it. First you crumple up newspaper, then you stack up little sticks like a teepee over it and—"

"Jimmy," his mother interrupted. "I wish I could bring you home with me right now. You know that, don't you?"

He nodded.

"It may be a little longer, but I'm going to bring you home with me soon. Okay?"

"Okay," he said.

"And things'll be a lot better than they were last time, I promise. I still had a lot of anger in me then, a lot of hurt. But I don't feel like that anymore. I've got a new outlook, and I'm going to make a better life for us. You'll see."

Jimmy looked at her. "You're not mad anymore?"

"No," she said, and Jimmy smiled. But then she added, "At least not like before. I'm learning to deal with it. It was hard at first, but it's getting easier."

Jimmy looked down then. She was still mad, she still had not forgiven him.

"At any rate," his mother continued, "Mrs. McClure says it won't be long before I can bring you back home."

Then she was silent. She was looking at the flames in the fireplace. One of the logs popped and some sparks struck the black mesh screen.

Jimmy knew he should say something, but he thought if he opened his mouth, he'd start to cry.

"The Kahlstroms have such a nice house," his mother said then. "I've always loved fireplaces. When I was a girl, I used to imagine the house I'd live in when I got married, and it always had a fireplace in it. And after dinner on cold winter nights my husband would build a big, roaring fire and we'd all sit around it and talk, the firelight flickering over our faces." She shook her head and laughed. It didn't sound like her laugh. And the things she was saying didn't sound like anything she'd ever said before. "I had it all figured out," she said. "I was going to have five children. I even had their names picked out—Joseph, Kevin, Abigail, Christine, and John, in that order. No James—that was your father's idea." She laughed again. "I had everything figured out. Every blessed thing." Then she turned her face toward him. There were tears in her eyes. "Don't you ever have everything figured out, you hear? Don't you—"

Then she couldn't talk anymore.

"What's wrong, Mom?" he managed to say.

"I'd better go," she said, and stood up. She took a crumpled Kleenex from her purse and wiped her eyes with it. "This was a mistake. I shouldn't be here." She looked around the room at the large-screen TV, the piano, the watercolor landscapes on the walls, the philodendron in the corner, and added, "I don't belong here."

"Don't go," he said, but it was too late: she was already on her way out.

"Tell Mr. and Mrs. Kahlstrom thank you for letting me come see you," she said as she put on her coat.

"Mom," he said. "Mom!"

She leaned over and took his face in her hands and kissed him. "My baby," she said.

And then she was out the door, and he was standing at the window, watching her walk carefully down the icy sidewalk through the falling snow, not even a scarf on her head, and Mr. and Mrs. Kahlstrom were coming down the stairs asking why she had left so soon. When he tried to answer, a sob rose into his throat and stuck. He shook his head, unable to speak.

Mrs. Kahlstrom put her hands on his shoulders. "Don't worry, honey. You'll see her again next week," she said, but he wrenched himself out of her hands and ran upstairs and locked himself in the bathroom. And although Mr. and Mrs. Kahlstrom stood outside the door and tried to comfort him, it was nearly an hour before he came out.

Mrs. Kahlstrom hugged him hard then and said they'd stay downstairs with him next time, if he wanted, so they could make sure his mother wouldn't upset him again. Jimmy didn't say anything for a long moment. Then he took a deep breath and said something he'd been wanting to say for the past four months. "If I get a job delivering papers, and save all my money, and pay for the windows, will Mrs. McClure let me go back home?"

"Windows?" Mrs. Kahlstrom said, then looked at her husband.

Mr. Kahlstrom wrinkled his forehead. "What windows, Jimmy? What are you talking about?"

And then he confessed it all.

Mr. Kahlstrom took Jimmy to see the high school counselor the next afternoon. His name was Mr. Sargent, but he told Jimmy to call him Ken. He was a skinny man with a ponytail, and he was wearing a corduroy sportcoat but no tie. He leaned back in his chair and put his scuffed Hush Puppies up on the desk. Behind him, on the wall, was a poster of a strangely dressed black man kneeling in front of a burning guitar. "So, Jimbo," he said, "what's a nice guy like you doing in a place like this?"

Jimmy sat there, looking down at his lap. His hands were shaking and he couldn't make them stop. He watched them tremble. Somehow, it seemed like it was happening a long way away, to somebody else maybe.

"You don't have to be afraid," Mr. Sargent said. "You can say anything in here. This is one place where you can say whatever you want. 'Cause I won't tell anyone anything you say. That's what 'confidential' means—you can be *confident* that I won't tell anyone your secrets."

Jimmy sat on his hands to make them stop. Then he tried to look up, but he couldn't. Finally, he said, "Did Mr. Kahlstrom tell you?"

"Tell me what, Jimbo?" Mr. Sargent said.

Jimmy didn't want to say. He was hoping Mr. Sargent didn't know.

"Tell me what?" Mr. Sargent asked again, more softly this time. "You can tell me."

"The windows," Jimmy managed to whisper.

"Oh, the *win*dows. Sure, he told me about the windows. But who cares about the lousy windows?"

77

Jimmy looked up, startled. Mr. Sargent smiled and went on. "It was wrong to break the windows, of course, but I don't have to tell you that—you already know it. But once they're broken, there's nothing you can do about it, except admit it like a man and say you're sorry and go on with your life. Everybody makes mistakes. That's how we learn to be better people. If we didn't make mistakes, we'd never learn anything. So think of it that way—as a mistake you made that you can learn from." Here he took his feet down from the desk and leaned forward in his chair. "What have you learned from all of this, Jimbo? Is there anything it's taught you that'll help you on down the road?"

Jimmy didn't think he'd learned anything, unless it was that he wasn't who he'd always thought he was. He didn't know who he was now, but he was someone else. Someone crazy, like his mother. And once Mr. Sargent found that out, he'd make him go to a hospital too.

"Let me guess, then," Mr. Sargent said. "You tell me if I'm getting warm, okay?" When Jimmy didn't respond, he repeated, "Okay?" Finally, Jimmy nodded. "All right, then. Did you learn that—hmm, let's see—that it's best to talk about your anger instead of breaking things?"

Jimmy hadn't been angry when he broke the windows, but he nodded yes anyway.

"Good. That's a good thing to learn. And did you also learn that secrets make you unhappy? That the longer you keep something inside, the more it hurts?"

Again Jimmy nodded, though he thought he hurt more now that people knew what he had done. And even though Mr. and Mrs. Kahlstrom told him he wasn't taken away from his mother because he broke the windows, he didn't know if he could believe them. They wanted him to like them, so maybe they would lie. And they wanted to adopt him, so maybe they would tell Mrs. McClure about the windows and Mrs. McClure would tell his mother, and then she'd say she couldn't take him back because she couldn't afford to pay for the windows like Mr. and Mrs. Kahlstrom could.

"That's good. That's very good. And did you maybe also learn how much people care about you? Because if they didn't, I wouldn't be here talking to you. I'm talking to you because *I* care, and because Mr. and Mrs. K care, and because everybody who knows you cares about you and wants you to be happy. Is that maybe something you learned from all of this, too?"

Jimmy looked at him, then at the floor. He didn't see the floor, though; he was seeing his father, the morning of the day he left for work and never came back, trimming his mustache in front of the bathroom mirror.

It took him longer this time, but once again he nodded.

The following Sunday, Mrs. McClure's Subaru pulled up in front of the Kahlstroms' house, but Jimmy's mother was not in it. "What a terrible day," Mrs. McClure said to the Kahlstroms, as she flicked the snow from her boots with her gloves. "We must have a foot of snow already." Then she cocked her head toward Jimmy. "I'm sorry, sweetie, but your mother isn't feeling well today. She said she'd try to come again next week. I hope you aren't too disappointed."

Jimmy said, "You told her, didn't you."

"Told her what?"

"You know."

"Oh, that. No, I didn't say anything. I told you I wouldn't tell, and I won't." Then she frowned. "Is that why you think she didn't come?"

"You can tell her if you want," he said, sticking his chin out. "She won't come anyway."

"Of course she will. She'll come tomorrow or the day after," Mrs. McClure said. "It's just that today—" But before she could finish, Jimmy turned and started to run up the stairs. "Jimmy!" she called after him. "Let me explain."

At the top of the stairs, he stopped and shouted down, "Tell her I don't care if she ever comes—not *ever!*" And then he ran into his room and slammed the door.

A few minutes later, he heard Mrs. McClure's car drive away, and then Mr. and Mrs. Kahlstrom came up and tried to talk to him. "We know you were looking forward to seeing her, honey," Mrs. Kahlstrom said, but he just dumped his entire canister of Legos onto the carpet and started putting them together.

"What're you building?" Mr. Kahlstrom asked.

"Nothing," he answered.

"Well," he said, "that shouldn't take much time." But Jimmy didn't laugh. Mr. Kahlstrom cleared his throat and looked at his wife. "Maybe we ought to let Jimmy be alone for a while," he said. Mrs. Kahlstrom nodded and said, "We'll be right downstairs if you need us. Okay, Jimmy?"

Jimmy didn't say anything. And when they left, he got up and closed the door again.

He tried to play with his Legos, but after a few minutes, he gave up and sat on the edge of his bed, looking out the window. It had been snowing all day, and now the snow was so thick he could barely see the houses across the street. He watched the evergreens sway in the yard and listened to the wind whistle in the eaves, then pressed his warm cheek against the windowpane. The window was cold and it vibrated a little with every gust of wind. It felt as if the glass were shivering, and for a second he thought it might even break. But he didn't move his face away; he pressed his cheek against it harder, until he could feel the cold right through to his cheekbone. He wished he were outside, walking through the waist-high drifts, the wind making his cheeks burn and his eyes tear; he wanted to be so cold that nothing could ever warm him up. That didn't make sense, but Jimmy didn't care if it did or not. He had a lot of thoughts he didn't understand, but he didn't worry about them anymore. You couldn't do anything about the brain that was in your head. Even if you were as rich as Michael Jackson, you still couldn't buy a new brain. You could get a new mother, but you couldn't get a new brain.

Later that night, Mr. Kahlstrom built a fire, and the three of them sat on the sofa eating popcorn and watching *E.T.* on videotape. The movie was sad, but Mr. and Mrs. Kahlstrom were smiling. It was so easy to make them happy, he thought; all he had to do was sit on the sofa with them. And that thought made him feel bad, because he had stayed in his room almost all day, making them worry.

Outside, the snow was still falling, a thick curtain of it, and every now and then the wind would rattle the windowpanes. "My, what a storm," Mrs. Kahlstrom said when the picture on the television flickered and went dark for a second. "We'd better get the candles out."

"It looks like we'll be snowed in tomorrow," Mr. Kahlstrom said. Then he tousled Jimmy's hair. "No school for us, eh buckaroo?"

Jimmy smiled and Mrs. Kahlstrom grinned. "I'd like that," she said. "We could sit around the fire and tell stories and play games, the way people did in the olden days. It'd be just like that poem 'Snow-Bound.' I memorized part of it when I was in high school, for a talent show." She lowered her head, as if it were immodest of her to say the word "talent." But then she began to half speak, half sing the poem:

> What matter how the night behaved?
> What matter how . . . the north-wind raved?
> Blow high, blow low, not all its snow
> Could quench our hearth-fire's ruddy glow.
> O Time and Change!—with hair as gray
> As was my father's—no, my *sire's*—that winter day,
> How strange it seems to still . . .

"No, that's not right," she broke off. "I think I missed a line in there somewhere."

"It sounded great to me," Mr. Kahlstrom said. "Go on. Recite some more for us." And he pressed the pause button on the remote control, freezing E.T. as he raised his glowing fingertip.

"All right," she said, "I'll see what else I can remember." Then she looked toward the ceiling as if the words were above her, floating through the air, like snowflakes.

> Ah, brother! only I and thou
> Are left of all that circle now—
> The dear . . . home faces whereupon
> That fitful firelight paled and shone.
> Henceforward, listen as we will,
> The voices of that hearth are still;
> Look where we may, the wide earth o'er,
> Those lighted faces smile no more . . .

She stopped abruptly and looked down at her lap. Mr. Kahlstrom reached across Jimmy and patted her hand. "It's all right, dear," he said. "Don't cry."

"I'm sorry," she said. "Sometimes I just remember and . . ."

"I know, dear. I do, too."

Jimmy looked at their faces. He wasn't sure what they were talking about. He hadn't understood the poem either, but he'd liked the way it made him feel warm and cold all at once, as if he had just come out of a blizzard to stand by a fire. He liked the way she'd said it, too, pronouncing each word as if it were almost too beautiful to say. And she'd had such a strange look on her face while she said it, kind of sad but in a way happy, too. He didn't know how you could be happy and sad at the same time. But now she only looked sad.

Just then the wind rose sharply and the television went black.

The only light left was the firelight. It cast long shadows up the walls around them, making Jimmy feel as if they were in a cave.

"I knew I should have gotten the candles out," Mrs. Kahlstrom said, and wiped her eyes.

"Don't worry, dear. I'm sure the electricity will be back on in no time. Let's just sit here and enjoy the fire."

He got up and threw two more logs on, adjusted them with the poker until the flames caught, then sat back on the sofa. "There," he said. "Isn't this cozy?"

They sat together a long time, watching the fire and talking. At first, Jimmy talked too, but after a while he started to grow tired and only listened to their quiet voices and the crackling fire and the wind. The way the wind battered the windows made the fire seem even warmer, and before long, Jimmy felt so drowsy and peaceful that he couldn't help but lean his head against Mrs. Kahlstrom's shoulder. She brushed his hair from his forehead while he listened to them talk and watched the fire through half-open eyes. Finally he couldn't keep his eyes open anymore, and he laid his head down in her lap and fell asleep.

When Jimmy woke the next morning, he was confused. It seemed as if only a moment before he'd been lying in front of the fire, and now he was upstairs in his room. How had it happened? Mr. Kahlstrom must have carried him up the steps and put him in his bed, but Jimmy didn't remember it. He felt as if a magician had made him disappear from one place, then reappear somewhere else. For a moment, he wasn't even sure he was the same person. He wondered if his mother had ever felt like that, waking up in the hospital, or if his father had the same thoughts when he sat down for breakfast with his new family. He didn't know, but he lay there awhile, thinking about it, before he got up and parted the curtains to look out the window. As far as he could see, everything was white—rooftops, the evergreens and yards, the street. The snow had drifted halfway up frosted picture windows and buried bushes and hedges and even the car parked in the neighbor's driveway. Here and there thin swirls of snow blew into the air like risen ghosts, and sunlight sparked on the drifts, the snow glinting like splintered glass. He'd never seen so much snow, not ever, and he wanted to run to Mr. and Mrs. Kahlstrom's room and tell them they were all snowbound, just like in the poem. But he stood there awhile longer, and imagined the huge fire they'd build, the yellow and orange flames rising up the chimney, and the three of them sitting beside it, unsure of what to say or even when to speak, but somehow strangely happy, their faces lit by a beautiful light.

Brutality

IT WAS LATE on a dark, moonless night, and they were driving home from a party at their friends' house on the other side of the city. Although they had been married for almost twenty years, Richard still loved Susan very much and found her attractive. At the party, he'd glanced at her across the room, and the way she crossed her legs when she sat down made him desire her. Now he was anxious to get home so they could make love. He thought she must be feeling the same way, for her hand was resting on his thigh and she was looking at him while they talked.

They were talking about their friends' little boy Joey, who had kept running in and out of the living room with a toy machine gun, pretending to shoot everybody. He had laughed like a crazed movie villain while he sprayed the room with bullets, the gun going ah-ah-ah and its muzzle glowing a fiery red. At first, everyone laughed too, but after the fourth or fifth time it stopped being funny. Finally, his father lost his temper, spanked Joey fiercely, and sent him crying to his room. Then his mother apologized to the guests. It was his grandmother's fault, she said; every time she came to visit, she brought him a gun. He had a half-dozen in his toybox, most of them broken, thank God. But the next time she visited, they were going to tell her they were opposed to children playing with guns. They would have told her earlier but they didn't want to hurt her feelings.

Richard and Susan had married during the Vietnam war and, like many parents then, didn't buy toy guns for their son. But Richard had played with guns when he was young, and now he was telling Susan about the rifle his father had carved for him out of an old canoe paddle. "I loved that rifle," he said, as he drove down the deserted street past the sleeping houses. It had been almost as long as a real rifle, and he had worn it slung over his shoulder wherever he went the summer he was nine. Even when his mother called him in for supper, he wouldn't put it away; he had to have it propped against the table in case the Russians suddenly attacked. As he thought about the rifle, its glossy varnish and its heft, he moved his hands on the steering wheel and could almost feel it again. A thin shiver of pleasure ran through him. "It was my favorite toy," he said wistfully. "I wonder what happened to it."

"I used to think it was so awful for kids to play war," Susan said, lifting her long dark hair off her neck and settling it over her shoulders. "But now I don't know. Look at this generation of kids that were raised without toy guns—they're all little Oliver Norths. They're playing with *real* guns now. And kids like you—you turned out all right. You wouldn't even think of going hunting, much less killing someone."

"At least not anymore," he said.

"What do you mean?" she said. "You mean you used to hunt?"

Susan was a vegetarian, and she did volunteer work on Saturdays for the Humane Society. Richard had told her many stories about his childhood—he had grown up in a small town in another state and didn't meet her until they were in college—but he hadn't told her he'd been a hunter. It wasn't that he considered that fact a dark secret; he just knew she'd be upset and didn't think it was worth telling her. He hadn't meant to mention it now either—it had just come out. Perhaps he'd drunk too much wine at the party. Or maybe he'd gotten so lost in his memories of the toy rifle that he spoke before he could think. Whatever, he didn't want an argument. He was in a romantic mood and he didn't want anything to destroy it.

"I was a kid," he explained. "I didn't know any better."

"How old were you?"

"What does it matter?" he said. "You know I wouldn't even kill a spider now."

"But you killed something then?"

He could lie now, he realized, and say he'd gone hunting but never shot anything. He could make up a story or two about his ineptitude as a hunter, and she would laugh and everything would be fine between them. But as he'd gotten older, lies had become harder for him. They had come easily to him in his youth, but now they tasted like rust in his mouth.

"Yes," he said.

She took her hand from his thigh and sat there silently. They passed under a streetlight, and her face flared into view. "Come on, Susan," he said. "Don't be mad."

Then she said, "How could you do it? Why would you even *want* to do it?"

It was a question he had asked himself from time to time. He had enjoyed hunting and trapping animals as a teenager, but now that he was an adult, he had no desire to do either. He thought of his brutality as a phase he had gone through, a period of hormonal confusion, perhaps, like puberty. But he still remembered the pleasure hunting and trapping gave him, and he still understood it.

"Do we have to talk about this?" he said.

"I want to know," she said.

He sighed. "Okay. If you really want to know, I did it because I wanted to see if I could hit something a long ways off." It was the simple truth. It was a thrill to shoot at the empty air half a sky in front of a pheasant or duck or goose and see that emptiness explode with the miraculous conjunction of bird and shot. It was a kind of triumph over chance, over the limitations of time and space, and each time it happened, he felt powerful and alive.

"But you could have shot at targets," she said.

"Targets don't move," he answered.

"What about clay pigeons? They move."

He wished they hadn't started this. "Can't we talk about something else?" he asked. He tried to make his voice as warm as he wished hers would be.

"First answer my question. Why not shoot at clay pigeons instead?"

He considered several lies while he turned onto the avenue that led toward the suburb where they lived. Then he sighed and said, "Because they aren't alive."

Susan looked at him. "I can't believe this," she said. "My own husband."

"Come on," Richard said. "You're overreacting."

"Maybe I am. But I feel like I'm seeing something in you that I never saw before."

"You're making me sound like a criminal or something," he complained.

"I think killing *is* a crime. It doesn't matter if it's an animal or a person, it's still murder."

He'd heard her make this argument many times before, but this was the first time she'd directed it at him personally. He wanted to defend himself, but even more he wanted to regain the romantic mood they were in when they left the party. He drove on in silence. Then she asked, "How did you feel when you killed something?"

He was glad this question had a more human answer. "I felt bad," he said. "I felt sorry for it."

"But you kept on hunting?"

"For a while."

"If you felt so sorry for the animals, why did you keep on killing them?"

He looked at her face then and knew he would have to tell her everything. If he didn't, she would never forgive him, and everything between them would be changed. He looked back at the road. "It may sound crazy," he said, "but the first time I shot something, I did it *because* I felt sorry for it."

"I don't understand."

"Do you want to?"

"Yes."

"All right then. I'll tell you the whole story." He took a breath. "The first real gun I owned was a .22 pistol. I was thirteen. I'd had the pistol for two or three months, and I'd never shot anything with it except Coke bottles and tin cans. I'd *tried* to shoot squirrels and birds, you understand, but I'd never hit anything. Then I met this boy. He was a couple of years older than me, and I looked up to him. Frank Elkington. He taught me to shoot and trap."

"Trap?" she said. "You trapped too? Richard, I just can't believe this is you you're talking about."

"It isn't. Not anymore."

"But it's who you were. And who you were is part of who you are, isn't it?"

He didn't like the way she was cross-examining him like a lawyer, and he thought about making some sarcastic joke about the statute of limitations. But he just stared straight ahead. They were driving through a business district now, and the reflections of neon lights crawled on the windshield. Finally he said, "I don't have to tell you this. I'm telling it because I love you."

"I know you do. And you know I love you."

He went on. "Frank trapped mink and muskrat and beaver along the Chippewa River and sold the pelts to a fur processing plant in town. I used to tag along with him when he did his paper route, and one day I went with him while he checked his traps. He was talking about trappers and how they lived off the land. They didn't breed animals just to slaughter them, he said, and they didn't keep them penned up either; they let the animals live free in the wild and gave them a sporting chance. He made it sound so noble that I told him I wanted to start trapping too. And he gave me my first trap."

He paused, remembering that trap. It was a rusty number eleven Victor Long-Spring, and it smelled oddly sulfurous, like the air just after a match is struck. Thinking of the trap did not give him the same pleasure that remembering the wooden rifle did, but it gave him some. He could not deny that.

"Frank showed me how to set the trap," he continued, "and the next day when we went to check it, there was a weasel in it." He paused again. "Are you sure you want to hear this?"

Susan's back was against the passenger door now and her arms were crossed over her breasts as if she were cold. She nodded.

"Okay. It was a black weasel. It wasn't worth much, but I was happy as hell. Frank was congratulating me, shaking my hand and patting me on the back, and I felt proud to have caught something on my first try, even if it was only a weasel. Then I noticed the weasel's mouth was bright red. I didn't understand at first, but then I saw its leg. It had started to chew the leg off, but we had gotten there before it could finish."

"Oh, Richard, that's awful," Susan said, and hugged herself tighter.

"I know. I know. I felt so sorry for that weasel I took out my pistol and shot him four or five times, to put him out of his misery. Frank yelled, 'What are you doing!' and grabbed the gun from me. 'You idiot,' he said, 'you're supposed to shoot it in the *head*. Now the pelt's *worthless*.'"

Richard could feel Susan looking at him, and he gripped the steering wheel a little harder. "That was the first animal I shot. The next one, I shot in the head, between the eyes, just to prove to Frank—and, I guess, to myself—that I could do it right."

"And you sold their fur?" she asked in a quiet voice.

"Yes. And that's how this farmer found out about me. Mr. Lyngen. He got my name from one of the men at the fur processing plant, and he hired me to trap gophers in his bean field. They were damaging his crop, and he didn't have time to trap them himself. He bought me a case of traps, and he gave me twenty cents a tail. By mid-summer, I'd earned enough to buy a .22 rifle, and by pheasant season I owned a 12 gauge shotgun too."

"You cut their tails off," she said. This time it was an accusation, not a question.

Yes, he had. When he'd found a gopher trapped in the entrance to its own burrow, he'd killed it with a single shot to the head, cut off its tail, then buried it in the grave it had dug for itself. He kept the tails in a marble bag tied to his belt, and every week or so when the bag got full, he took it to Mr. Lyngen and collected his bounty.

Neither of them said anything for a moment. Then Susan said, "What made you stop?"

"Another trapper. A kid named Jake Weckworth. I'd been trapping for a couple of years when he moved to town, and he started trapping too. One morning I went to check my traps, and they were missing. I didn't know who'd taken them, but I suspected Jake. A few days later, I found the traps set along a creek that ran into the river. I'd scratched my initials into them with a nail, but Jake had filed them off and scratched his own in. I collected the traps and took them to Jake's house and showed his father what he'd done. That afternoon, Mr. Weckworth brought Jake to my house and made him apologize. Jake mumbled he was sorry, and his father gripped his arm and said, 'Say it louder.' So he said it again. I could tell Jake was mad: his jaw muscles were working, and he wouldn't look at me. But I never expected anything to come of it." He paused. "I was wrong, of course. The next morning, when

I went down to the river to set my traps, he was there waiting for me."

"Did he beat you up?" Susan asked.

Richard shook his head. "No. Not really. Mostly, he just threatened me. I was walking along the river, looking for good places to set my traps, and all of a sudden he just stepped out from behind a tree and pointed his 12 gauge at me. I stopped dead. Then he said, 'Hello, Richie,' and smiled. For a second I thought he wasn't going to do anything. But then he stuck the muzzle of his shotgun against my throat. 'I ought to kill you,' he said, and poked me with the shotgun, hard. And he kept on poking me until I was crying and gasping for breath."

It had happened twenty-five years ago, but as he described it, he could feel the cold steel against the soft flesh under his Adam's apple. He touched his throat gingerly with his fingertips as he steered the car through the dark tunnel formed by the huge oaks that lined the street. In a few minutes, they'd be home. In a few minutes, he'd walk into his house, a grown man with a son who was himself almost grown. It seemed amazing that all these years had passed and, at the same time, somehow not passed too.

"That's terrible," Susan said. "What happened then?"

"Not much. He took the traps back and warned me not to tell his father or ever show my face in the woods again. If I did, he said, he'd kill me."

"He couldn't have meant it," she said. "He must have just been trying to scare you."

Richard thought for a moment. "Probably. But I don't know. He looked like he meant it." He turned to Susan. "There was something in his eyes. It may sound strange, but it was something like fear. Not fear exactly, but close to it. I remember thinking, Here he is, the one with the gun, and he's afraid."

"Afraid of what?"

He looked away. "I'm not sure. Afraid he might actually do it, I think. Afraid he was capable of it. Maybe even afraid he'd *enjoy* it."

He didn't know whether he should say anything more. Then he did. "I wanted to kill him, Susan." And as he said those words, he remembered picturing Jake dead, his face turned to pulp by a shotgun blast, and for an instant he felt again the comfort and pleasure that thought had given him then. Leaning back in his seat, he let out a slow breath. Then he continued. "I never did it, of course, but I thought about it for weeks. And night after night, I dreamed about it. I must have killed him a hundred times in my dreams."

Susan was silent. He waited for her to say something, and when she didn't, he turned to look at her. He had thought she was punishing him with her silence, thinking thoughts she didn't dare let bleed into words, and he expected to see her glaring at him, her face a mask of anger and disgust. But even in the dark, her face looked pale, and she was wincing as if his words had wounded her. "Susan?" he said. And then she put her hands over her face and began to cry.

Richard turned away. He had tolerated her self-righteous questions, but her tears angered him. She wasn't crying for him and what he had gone through; she was crying for herself, pitying herself for having married a man who had once killed animals and dreamed about killing a human being. She had no right to take his past so personally. It was his past, not hers. And she had no right to judge him.

"In one dream," he went on, his voice thick with a bitterness that was directed more at her now than at Jake, "I trapped him just like an animal. His foot was caught in the trap, and he couldn't get it out. He kept asking me to let him go, but I just—"

"Stop it," Susan said. "Please stop it."

And then he was ashamed of hurting her, and of wanting to

hurt her. He cleared his throat. "I'm sorry," he said. "I just don't want you to—" But he couldn't explain. He sighed, then drove on without talking for a while. When he finally spoke, his voice was gentle. "I know it's awful even to think about killing someone," he said, "and I don't know why I did it. I've never felt that way about anyone else, not ever. All I know is that it wasn't real, it was just a fantasy. I never really considered doing it." He glanced at her. "You know that, don't you?"

She was drying her eyes with a Kleenex. She nodded.

"At any rate, that was the end of my hunting and trapping. I never went back to the woods, and the next time my mom had a garage sale, I sold the rest of my traps and all my guns."

He looked at her and tried a smile. "That's it," he said. "The whole story. The End. *Fini.*"

She didn't return his smile. "I've never wanted to kill anything," she said. "I can't imagine feeling that way." Then she added, almost as if she were talking to herself, "It makes me wonder. What if he hadn't threatened you? Would you have kept on hunting and trapping? Would you be the same person you are now? Would you even be married to me?"

"You're making too much of this," he said. "It happened years ago. I didn't even know you then."

"I know," she said.

"It was a big mistake to tell you this," he said. "I shouldn't have said anything."

"Don't feel bad," Susan said. "I don't mean to make you feel bad. It's just that I never thought of you like this before. I always thought you were different from the kind of people who hunt and trap."

"I *am.*"

"I know. I just had too much to drink tonight, and I'm taking everything too serious. I'll feel fine tomorrow."

"Good," he said. "I'm glad to hear that."

Then they were out of words. They drove the last few blocks in silence, and when he had parked the car in their garage, they got out and went quietly into the house. Stepping softly so they wouldn't wake their son, they went down the hall to their bedroom. There, they undressed slowly in the dark, then put on their pajamas, got into bed, and lay on their backs, breathing quietly. Susan's hand was lying palm down on the sheet beside him, and he traced its small bones lightly with a fingertip. After a while, she moved her hand away. "Goodnight," she said, and turned her back to him.

Richard lay there for a long time, looking at the dark ceiling. He could tell by Susan's breathing that she was still awake, but he knew she didn't want to make love now, or even talk, so he didn't say anything. But after a few more minutes, he couldn't bear the silence anymore. Turning to her, he said, "I love you."

"I love you too," she answered.

But still she kept her back to him. He lay there on his side, facing her rigid back, awhile longer, until the distance between them was too much of an affront. Then he put his hand on her shoulder and, whispering her name, turned her beautiful body toward him.

The Late Man

I T H A D B E E N a bad day. Dana and I had a terrible fight that afternoon, our worst one ever, and I got so angry that I raised my fist as if to hit her. I didn't, but to her it was the same as if I had. She called me a wifebeater and told me to get out. I'd had more than enough by then, so I turned and stormed out of the house, slamming the door behind me. Then I saw Amy sitting on her Big Wheels in the carport, crying, and I realized she'd heard us fighting. "Don't cry, sweetheart," I said. "There's nothing to cry about." But she kept on, her little chin quivering, so I told her I was going to the store and would bring her back some cherry popsicles, her favorite treat. Normally she would have smiled, maybe even clapped her hands, but that day she just kept on crying. "I'll be right back," I said then, and left.

But I didn't come back right away. I drove around for a couple of hours, not going anywhere particular, just driving and thinking things out. When I'd finally cooled off, I picked up a box of popsicles and some other groceries at Safeway and started back home. But when I turned onto our block, I don't know, suddenly I felt as if I couldn't even look at our house. I just wanted to drive on by, as if

I'd never lived there and didn't know anybody who did. I wanted to drive and drive until I was in another life. I saw myself somewhere far away, in Canada maybe, pulling into a motel late at night, the groceries still on the seat beside me. And I *did* drive by. I passed Amy on her Big Wheels and didn't even wave, and I felt then the sudden pleasure of conclusion, of closing accounts, the clean pure thrill of zero. By the time that feeling faded and I turned back toward home again, the popsicles were a red puddle on the carseat.

When I got home, Dana and I fought again, and by that night, when I had to go to work, my mind was a whirl of anger and confusion. As the *Courier*'s late man, I was responsible for proofing each page before sending it on to camera, but I was too upset to concentrate and I held up the production schedule so much that it was an hour after deadline before we turned the state edition. Even if a big story hadn't come in over the wire just before deadline—a plane had crashed in Detroit, killing everyone on board except a four-year-old girl named Cecelia Cichan—we would have turned late. Still, I hoped I could use that story to convince the managing editor to give me another chance. I knew he'd call me in his office the next day, and when he asked me what my excuse was this time, I'd tell him we'd had to re-do page one to get the story on, and how that meant we had to move our lead story down below the fold, move another story inside, and revise the jump pages. I hoped that would convince him not to fire me, but I doubted it would.

We'd turned the state edition so late I had to run three red lights to get to the Burger Palace before they closed at ten. The Burger Palace was the only restaurant downtown that stayed open Sunday nights, mostly for those of us at the *Courier* and the *Herald*, the rival paper, and by the time I pulled into its lot, the sign had already been turned off. But two employees were still behind the counter and there was a customer sitting in one of the booths, so I knew I'd made it in time. I sat there in the car for a second, my heart still speeding, then got out and started toward the door.

I was in a bad enough mood, but as soon as I stepped into the restaurant and heard steel guitars and a cowboy's nasal twang, I felt worse. The waitresses had the radio turned to KABX, the country station. I'd lost a dozen accounts to that station when I worked for KEZN, and I still couldn't listen to it without anger. The way I saw it, KEZN was responsible for the problems Dana and I were having. After they fired me, she had to go on overtime at the beauty shop, and we didn't see much of each other anymore. And when we did, we were in such miserable moods—me, because I wasn't working; her, because she was working so much—that we fought more than usual. And now things had gotten so bad that I'd almost left her and Amy.

I stepped up to the cash register, trying to ignore the music, and one of the waitresses came over to help me. She was around my age, but she looked younger, partly because she was tiny and partly because she wore her blonde hair pulled back into a ponytail. The nametag pinned to her red, white, and blue striped shirt said "Monica." She smiled when she said hello, and I decided she was pretty.

"You just made it," she said. "Carol Sue's locking up now."

I glanced over my shoulder and saw that the other waitress, a sullen-looking teenager with greasy brown hair and acne, had come around the counter and was turning the key in the lock.

"Guess this is my lucky night," I said, just barely keeping the sarcasm out of my voice. Then I ordered king burgers with fries for myself and the copy editors. They were back in the newsroom, scrolling the wire and subbing out state stories for the city edition, and when I brought them their food, they'd have to keep working at the terminals while they ate. I knew they blamed me for making them work through their dinner break, and I was certain they were complaining about me that very minute.

As Monica rang up the order, I heard a curse from behind me and turned to look. The customer I'd seen earlier had spilled some french fries on her lap. She slid out of her booth, mumbling, a cigarette in one hand, and brushed the fries and salt from her loose Hawaiian print dress with her free hand. She was a short, heavy-breasted black woman, maybe thirty-five or forty years old, and she was so drunk she could hardly stand. Her eyes were half-closed, and she tilted her head back as if to help her see through the slits. She looked toward me. "What you looking at?" she said. I'd heard drunks say that before, but she said it differently, as if she wasn't so much angry as curious. Before I could say anything, she waved her hand, as if to erase her question, and said, "Just a minute." Then she leaned over her table, bracing herself with one hand so she wouldn't fall, and picked up a large green vinyl purse. Turning, she staggered toward the counter. I smelled the liquor on her breath before she reached me.

"Hi," she slurred, almost giving the word a second syllable. Then she stumbled and fell against me, her shoulder against my arm, her hip against my thigh. "Esscuse me," she said, but she didn't move away. She just closed her eyes and rested her head on my shoulder. For a moment I wondered whether she was a prostitute. But she was so ugly she would have had a hard time making a living on her back. Her leathery skin, broad, flat nose, and large mouth all made me think of some kind of lizard or salamander. I cleared my throat. It was a kind of speech, and evidently she understood because she shifted away from me and leaned against the counter for balance. I glanced at Monica. She rolled her eyes, then gave me my change and went back into the kitchen.

The black woman took a drag on her cigarette and blew tusks of smoke out her nostrils. Then she closed her eyes for a long moment. When she finally opened them, she handed the cigarette to me.

"Here," she said woozily. "Hold this for me."

I didn't want to be bothered with her, but I didn't know what to do, so I took it.

She started to fumble with the worn gilt clasp on her purse. "Come on, purse," she mumbled. "Open up."

I was feeling foolish holding the cigarette, so I set it on the counter, letting the long ash hang over the edge. It wouldn't have taken much to hold her cigarette for a moment or two, but I didn't.

Then she got her purse open and stood there swaying and looking into it as if it were so deep she couldn't see to the bottom. "There it be," she finally said, and pulled out an almost empty pint of George Dickel. She held the bottle out toward me, closed her eyes, and said, "Want a drink?"

"No thank you," I said. Then I cleared my throat again and said I had to go. I wanted to sit down at one of the booths and relax, smoke a cigarette or two. But as soon as I started toward the booths, she took hold of my arm and said, slowly, as if each word were a heavy weight, "Ain't you my friend?"

I didn't know what to say, so I just stood there. She let go of my arm and put the bottle to her lips. When she finished, there was only a swallow left. "What's your name?" she said.

"Paul," I said. I don't know why I didn't tell her my real name. It wouldn't have cost me anything.

She moved her face toward me then, as if to see me better, and I saw her red, swollen eyes. That's when it struck me that maybe she wasn't just a drunk. Her eyes looked like Dana's had that afternoon, when I came home after our argument. "My name's Lucy," she said, her eyes closing. She seemed to have to force them open again. Then she said, "My boy is dead."

I wasn't sure I'd heard her right. "Pardon me?"

"My boy . . ." Then she saw the cigarette on the counter and carefully, as if her fingers were somehow separate from her, picked it up and put it in her mouth, though she did not take a puff. "He died today. My boy. My Freddie."

I heard a voice from the kitchen then. "Here she goes again," it said.

I looked toward the booths. "I'm sorry," I said. But I'm not sure it was true. Mostly, I felt uncomfortable. I wanted to get my burgers and go.

"That's nice," she said, and leaned against me again. "You're nice." Then she straightened up and smiled at me. When she did, her cigarette dropped to the floor. She stared at it a moment, then looked back at me. "What did you say?" she asked.

"Nothing," I said.

"I thought you said something," she said. Then she tilted her head back and swallowed the last of her bourbon. She held the bottle to her thick lips for a long time, tapping the bottom with her finger. When she finally set the bottle on the counter, she looked at me and said, "Empty."

I nodded and glanced over at the booths. Then she grabbed my arm again. "Please," she said urgently. "Don't leave me alone. I been alone all day and I can't take it no more."

Her fingers were pressing into my skin, but I didn't pull my arm away.

"I'm sorry," I said again.

She shook her head slowly. "He was only thirteen. His voice was still changing." Her lips started to tremble. "One minute it was high, then the next . . ." She stopped and tears began running out of the slits of her eyes.

I looked around for the waitresses, but they were still in the kitchen. I heard the sizzle of the grill through the nasal whine of a country singer complaining about his woman running around. I wished they would hurry up.

"Have you talked to someone?" I asked. I meant a minister or a doctor, but I don't think she understood.

"He won't talk to me," she said. "He blame me for it all. He say I the one made Freddie do it, I the one after him all the time to do his schoolwork, clean his room." She squeezed her eyes shut.

I could have asked "Do what?" but I already knew. Now I wanted more than ever to get away from her and her grief.

"Excuse me," I said, and pulled my arm out of her grip. "I need to go sit down."

She followed me toward the booth, talking to my back. "I beg him not to do it," she said. "I beg him and beg him, but he say 'Go away and leave me be or I do it now.' And when I reach out for him, he do it. My boy, he *do* it." Then a sob shuddered through her.

It may sound strange, but I was embarrassed by her grief. I felt sorry for her, I truly did, but I was embarrassed too. Maybe it was because she was a stranger and I couldn't possibly share her grief. Or maybe it was because her grief had taken her so far beyond embarrassment that I felt some odd obligation to be embarrassed for her. I don't know. All I know for sure is that I wanted to get away from her more than I wanted to comfort her.

I started toward the men's room. "Where you going?" she asked.

"I can't help you," I answered, more bluntly than I intended, then went in the men's room and locked the door behind me.

"What's wrong?" she said. She knocked on the door. "What'd I do?"

"Nothing," I said. But the way I said it I might as well have said, "Go away." Then, her voice wavering, she started talking about her son again.

I looked around the room and tried not to listen. The walls were covered with graffiti—phone numbers, drawings of naked women and penises, a dirty limerick or two—and where a mirror had once hung over the sink someone had written on the bare plasterboard KEEP AMERICA BEAUTIFUL and, underneath, KILL ALL THE NIGGERS. I thought about all the blacks who came into that room and read those words, and I looked back at the door. The woman was saying something about a bridge then, and that's when I remembered the story. A teenaged boy, a student at Emerson Junior High, had climbed out onto the ledge of an old railway bridge and dove to the rocks below. But it hadn't happened that day, as she'd said; it had happened at least two weeks ago. I remembered proofing the story. It'd been too long to fit the hole in our Police Beat section, so I'd had to cut the last paragraph, which mentioned that the boy's parents witnessed the suicide.

"Cars be going by," she was half saying, half sobbing, "but nobody is stopping, everybody is just looking out at us. One of them even points at us like we are something *interesting*. And I say, I say, 'Freddie, come back, everything be all right,' and he say, 'No, Mama,' and I reach out for him but he just lean forward. He just lean forward and I feel him going like it is me going and oh, his sweet head, his sweet, sweet head!"

I opened the door. She was standing there, swaying back and forth and holding her head as if it were about to shatter.

"I'm sorry," I said. And I *was* sorry for her. But even more I was sorry for my failure to comfort her. What I felt was more shame than sympathy, and later, when I realized that, I felt even greater shame.

"Ohhh," the woman moaned, then slumped into one of the booths. She put her face down on the tabletop and covered her head with her hands, like a soldier under fire.

The younger waitress—Carol Sue—appeared at the counter then with a white paper bag. "Sir, your order's ready," she said.

As sorry as I felt for the woman, I was glad to have an excuse to leave. I stepped up to the counter and took the bag. Looking over my shoulder, Carol Sue said, "Excuse me, ma'am, but we have to close up now." Then she came out from behind the counter with a ringful of keys in her hand.

The woman gradually stood up. She wasn't crying anymore. "I ain't got nowhere to go," she said.

"You can go home, can't you?" Carol Sue said, biting down on the words. "You do have a home, don't you?"

The woman shook her head. "No. Not no more."

Monica came out of the kitchen then, wiping her hands on a

towel. She smiled in a stiff, controlled way that didn't reach her eyes. "Is there someone we can call for you?" she asked the woman. "Or a taxi?"

"Ain't no one," the woman said.

By this time I was at the door, waiting for Carol Sue to unlock it. I turned my back to Monica and the woman and tried to listen to the radio. But still I heard Monica say *I'm sorry but* and *police*. Then Carol Sue turned the key in the lock, and I hurried out to my car, opened the door, and jumped in. As I put the key in the ignition, the woman stumbled out of the Burger Palace and ran toward me. "Wait," she said. "Stop."

But I didn't wait. I started the car and began to back up. She ran up alongside the car and knocked on the passenger window. "Help me," she said. As I stopped to shift into drive, she put her face up to the window, her wet cheeks glistening in the light cast by the streetlight. "*Please*," she said. And she leaned against the car as if it were all that was holding her up.

I could have shifted into park. I could have rolled down the window and asked what she wanted. I could have talked with her for a few minutes or even offered to give her a ride. I could have put my arms around her and consoled her the best I was able. But what I did was reach over and lock the door.

She stood up then and watched me as I turned around and headed out of the lot. I looked in the rearview mirror and saw her standing there in the middle of the black asphalt. Then I turned onto Calhoun and pressed on the accelerator.

As I drove down the street, I once again imagined driving away from everything. I saw myself on the freeway, driving in my dark car through the anonymous night, on my way to a new life, a new self. But this time that thought didn't give me any pleasure. This time it scared me.

When I turned down Fremont and saw the *Courier* building looming in the dark, I accelerated and sped past the turnoff to the parking lot. I wasn't sure where I was going. For a moment, I thought about going back to the Burger Palace and comforting the woman—*Lucy*, I told myself, *her name is Lucy*—but I didn't. Why didn't I go back? Part of it, I'm ashamed to say, was that she was black. I asked myself, would I have comforted her if she were someone else? What if she were white, and pretty? What if she were Monica? Or what if she were *Dana*? And then I saw Dana in the Burger Palace, drunk and staggering up to a stranger to tell him her life was ruined, and I felt something narrow inside me open wide, like a wound.

But still I did not go back to the restaurant that night. I went there the next three nights and then occasionally after that, but I never saw Lucy again. I asked Monica and Carol Sue about her, but they didn't know any more than I did. I thought of checking the police report for her address, but I didn't. I still think about doing it, sometimes, though I know I never will. It wouldn't make much difference now. Whatever I said or did would be too late to help.

I didn't go back to the *Courier* that night either. Instead, I went home. At first I didn't realize that was what I was doing, and when I found myself turning onto our street, I thought I must have done it through force of habit. But it wasn't habit. It was something like habit, only deeper and more powerful. Whatever it was, it's what I most miss, now that Dana and I are divorced.

When I went inside, Dana was in the kitchen, washing dishes. She turned when she heard me, and I saw that she'd been crying again. Her eyes were red, and there were some Kleenexes crumpled on the counter beside her.

I stopped next to the refrigerator. On it, held up by magnets, was a picture Amy had drawn of a purple flower with a smiling face.

Dana pushed a strand of her black hair behind her ear with the back of a wet hand. "You're awfully early," she said.

"I'm not fired, if that's what you're thinking. I just came home

105

for a minute. I'm going right back." I still didn't know why I'd come home; I only knew that I'd had to.

"Good," she said, wiping a plate with the washcloth.

"Let's not fight," I said.

"Who's fighting? If I state a simple fact, does it mean I'm fighting?"

"No."

"Okay. Then leave me alone."

She kept on washing dishes and stacking them in the rack. I watched for a moment, then cleared my throat. "You've been crying," I said.

"Very observant of you."

"Please," I said. "Don't."

She whirled toward me then, her face red and pinched and her lips quivering. "Don't what?" she said, her voice rising. "Don't hit you? Don't yell at you? Don't make our daughter cry?"

I didn't say anything. She turned back to the sink and began violently scrubbing a pot. "Just leave me alone, will you," she said. "Just go away and leave me in peace. Leave us both in peace."

"Is that what you want?" I said.

"That's what I want."

I felt groggy, as if I were just waking up. "You mean, you want a divorce?"

"Yes," she said. "I do."

I didn't know what to say. I just stood there, watching her back. Then I heard Amy's footsteps in the hall.

"Mama," she called.

I looked at the doorway and there she was, standing in her pink pajamas, rubbing her eyes.

"Hello, honey," I said, and went over and squatted down beside her. There was a pillow print running down her cheek like a scar. I kissed it and, as I did, heard Lucy saying "his sweet, sweet head."

I made myself smile. "What are you doing up so late, little lady?"

"A dog was chasing me," she said. She spread her arms wide. "A *big* dog. And he was *barking* at me."

"It's just a dream," Dana said, wiping her hands on a dishtowel. "I'll take you back to bed, sweetheart."

"That's okay," I said. "I'll do it." And I hoisted her up and carried her back into her dark bedroom and tucked her in. Then I brushed her hair away from her eyes and kissed her forehead. Fear was feathering in my chest, making it hard for me to breathe. I knew this might be the last time I'd tuck my daughter into bed in this house. "Good night, honeybunch," I said.

"What if he comes back?" Amy said then.

"If he comes back," I said, "I'll chase him away."

"Don't hit him, though," she said. "I don't think he means to be mean."

"Okay," I said, and kissed her on the nose. Then I went back into the kitchen.

"Don't you think you'd better get back to work?" Dana said. She was still doing dishes, her arms sunk almost to her elbows in the sudsy water.

I thought about the bag of food in the car and imagined the copy editors checking their watches and cursing me for taking so long. "Yes," I said. But I didn't move.

Dana kept on doing the dishes as if I weren't there. I watched her for a long moment, and I thought about Lucy and wondered where she was. Then I said, "I'm sorry."

She didn't say anything; she just shook her head. I wanted to walk up behind her then and take her into my arms. I wanted to tell her I loved her. I wasn't sure it was true, at least not anymore, but it had been once and maybe it would be again. There were so many things I wanted to say, but my thoughts withered to one word. "Dana," I said.

"I don't want to talk about it now," she said. "Just go, and we'll talk about it later."

Something funny happened then. I don't know why—maybe it was because I was thinking about going back to the *Courier*—but I suddenly saw that plane going down in Detroit—not just the words of the story, the black ink, the typos and style errors, but the plane itself. I saw it rock back and forth, then begin to plunge, saw the left wing strike the Avis building, shearing stone into sparks, and the plane skid, streaming fire, beneath the railroad trestle and the interstate overpass. And through it all I saw the terrified faces in the fiery windows.

I felt lightheaded, dizzy, as if I'd drunk the bourbon Lucy had offered me. I had to do something or I'd start to shake, so I stepped up to the sink and took Dana's arm. She turned and looked at me, her lips set in a hard thin line. I knew then that it was too late to change her mind, but there was something I had to say, something I had to make her understand, though I didn't know what it was myself until I'd already said it.

"There's been a terrible accident," I said. And my voice shook as if I were breaking the news about a death in the family.

Rainier

WHEN Barbara called to tell me about Chuck, I was so drunk I said, "Chuck who?" Then she knew I'd started back drinking again.

"Damn it, Alec," she said. "You're *drunk*."

I said no, I hadn't been drinking, only a small glass of champagne with dinner. Then she started to cry.

"Don't cry," I said. "I won't drink anymore, I promise." I was feeling awful. Only a month before, I'd mailed her a Xerox copy of my diploma from Intercept, the alcoholic treatment center in Missoula. I sent it to her because she spent half our marriage trying to get me to go there and I wanted to show her I'd finally done it. Maybe I wanted to make her feel a little sorry for me too, like if she'd stayed with me a few more years everything would have worked out. But now she knew I was drinking again. "Please don't cry," I said.

"You stupid drunk," she answered. "I'm not crying about *you*." Then she hung up.

It wasn't until then, I think, that I understood what she'd said about Chuck. I don't know why it took so long to sink in. I mean, I was drunk, but not that drunk.

I sat there in the kitchen holding the phone for a minute, then went into the living room and turned on the TV. I wasn't going to watch; I just wanted the noise. I sat down in the La-Z-Boy and picked up the bottle of Cold Duck from the coffee table and took a slug. It was warm and flat. I took another slug and laid my head back and closed my eyes. But that didn't work, so I got up and started walking around the apartment. I thought about getting out my tool box and planing down the closet door that stuck. I thought about calling Betty, my new girl. I even thought about trying to sew up the old tear in the bedroom drapes. But I just stood there by the window and watched the snow fall. It was coming down in such big soft flakes it almost looked fake. Down the street, the Greyhound sign flickered, slowly shorting out. I knocked back the last of the Cold Duck, then sat on the edge of the bed, staring out the window.

After a while, I went back into the kitchen. There was no more champagne in the fridge but I had some Early Times in the cupboard. When I took it down, I noticed the blender on the shelf above it. It was avocado-colored, the same as the fridge and stove Barbara and I used to have. I'd bought it for her on one of our wedding anniversaries, but she forgot to take it when she cleaned me out after the divorce. I'd never used it, even once, so I took it down and turned it on, trying all the buttons. Chop. Puree. Blend. It worked like new.

Later, I called Barbara back. Her new husband answered the phone, his voice hoarse, like he'd been crying or had just woken up. I'd never met him. All I knew about him was the little Barbara had told me: that he was a geologist at the oil camp outside of Rose Creek, and that he was a good father to Chuck. When Chuck graduated from Officers' Training School, Barbara sent me a picture of him in his dress blues, standing between two men in civilian clothes. One of them was lanky and stoop-shouldered; the other, squat and red-faced. On the back of the picture, Barbara had written "Ensign Charles F. Denton, with Gale and Uncle Zack." I knew Gale was her new husband's name, but I didn't know which one was him. I tried to imagine each of them making love to Barbara, but I couldn't. I couldn't imagine them tousling Chuck's hair or taking him trout fishing either. So I didn't know who I was talking to. "Hello," I said to him, whichever one he was. "This is Alec."

Then he said, "Yeah? Alec *who*?" and I knew Barbara had told him what I'd said. I didn't blame him for hating me. I would've felt the same way if I was him.

"Listen," I said, "I'm sorry. I was drunk when Barbara called. I was out of my mind. She threw me for a loop. But I'm not drunk now and I want to say I feel awful and I want to be there with you and Barbara now. Maybe I don't deserve to be there, but I need to." I stopped, but he didn't say anything. I was afraid he was going to hang up on me. "Mr. Denton?" I said. "Are you still there?" He didn't answer. I closed my eyes and listened to the three hundred miles of silence between us. "I just need to see him," I said.

When he finally answered, I decided he was the lanky stoop-shouldered man who was standing on Chuck's left. "All right," he said. "Of course you can come. After all, you were his father too."

There's not much you can do in a car except think. During the long drive from Bozeman to Rose Creek, I kept a twelve-pack beside me, and every now and then I drank a can. I listened to the radio too, when I could stand the sort of music they play on it these days, and watched the wipers clean the snow from the windshield until I was half-hypnotized. I even kept track of the gas I bought and the distance I drove, so I could figure out how many miles per gallon the old Nova was getting. But no matter what I did, I kept thinking about Chuck. I remembered the strangest things. Like those Hawaiian swimtrunks he had—"jams" he called them—with yellow and maroon flowers. The time he fell off his skateboard and broke his collarbone. The way he once did a drumroll with his fork and knife when Barbara set supper on the table.

But mostly I kept remembering the lie I told Chuck about Mount Rainier. I hadn't thought about it for years. Chuck had just turned twelve, but I hadn't been home for his birthday. I'd been gone for four days, drinking, and when I came home he wouldn't even talk to me. I said, "Your dad's home" and he looked away; I said, "Are you mad at me?" and he ran back to his room. I'd been gone on binges before, but never that long, and never over his birthday. I felt so miserable I went back to his room and told him I'd take him out to Mount Blackmore the next day. He'd been begging me for weeks to take him there so he could earn his mountain climbing merit badge, but when I told him I'd take him, he didn't look happy or anything. And the next day, when we hiked up the mountain, I couldn't get him to talk. I'd say something about the trees or rocks—ask him what kind he thought they were and things like that—and he'd just answer with a word or two. So by the time we were halfway up the trail, I was getting scared that this time he wasn't going to forgive me.

So I told him the lie. We were taking a breather, sitting on a big slate ledge in the sun, looking down at the creek at the base of the bluff and the pine woods beyond, and I told him I had once climbed Mount Rainier. Chuck looked at me then, but he didn't say anything.

"This was a long time ago," I said. "Long before you were born. Even before I met your mother." Then I told him a friend and I had gone up the mountain in the winter of '51. "Everything went fine," I said, "until we got halfway up the mountain. Then the wind kicked up and snow began to fall and pretty soon we were caught in a first-class blizzard. We couldn't see anything, the snow was so thick, and the air was so cold it burned our lungs just to breathe. Before long the wind was blowing to beat Billy Hell and we could barely hang on to the side of the mountain, even with our spiked boots dug in." I went on to tell him we knew we'd freeze to death if we didn't get up to the next ledge and dig a snow cave, so we kept climbing, feeling our way up the mountain inch by inch like blind men.

The story was a true one, but it hadn't happened to me—I'd read about it in *Reader's Digest*. But I told it like it was my story, not somebody else's, and Chuck sat there looking out toward the horizon, his forehead creased like he was thinking hard. And as I told the story, I got excited and started to make up things that weren't even in *Reader's Digest*. I told him my friend fell and broke his leg so I had to strap him onto my back and lug him up the ridge with me, and I told him we were trapped there for three days before the weather cleared enough for me to carry him back down the mountain. I even told him my name had been in all the papers and the governor of Washington himself came to the hospital where I was recuperating to shake my hand and congratulate me for saving my friend's life.

I'd hoped my story would make Chuck proud of me, make him forgive me for being a drunk and a bad father. But he didn't say anything. He just sat there, looking down at his boots. I figured he knew I was lying, and was even madder than before. But then I saw that his lower lip was trembling.

"What's wrong?" I said.

"You could have died," he answered.

When he said that, I thought maybe I had won him back after all. "That's right," I said. "I could've died. But I didn't." And I tousled his curly blond hair.

But he kept looking at his boots. "But what if you *had* died?"

I tried to laugh it off. "Then I would've died," I said, and punched him lightly on the shoulder.

He reached down then and picked up a small stone and flicked it off the cliff. We watched it hit a ledge below and bounce off out of sight.

"Then I wouldn't have been born," he said.

I was wrong about Barbara's new husband. He wasn't the tall stoop-shouldered guy after all. He was the squat meaty-faced fellow with thick glasses. He didn't look at all like the type Barbara would marry, but then again neither did the tall lanky guy. And, I suppose, neither did I.

"You must be Alec," he said, when he opened the door. "I'm Gale. Come on in. It must be freezing out there."

I'd never met a man named Gale before. "Gale" seemed like a woman's name to me, even though it was spelled different, and I'd never liked the fact that Barbara had married someone with a name like that. I shook his hand. "Pleased to meet you, Mr. Denton," I said, and stepped in the house.

It was a nice house, a lot nicer than any house Barbara and I ever lived in. To the right of the entryway was a living room with a red brick fireplace and a blue and gold Oriental rug, and straight down the hall there was a dining room with a chandelier tiered like an upside-down wedding cake. To my left, there was a short flight of stairs that led up to a hallway of rooms. Everywhere you looked there were plants and fancy paintings. I felt like I was stepping into a copy of *Better Homes and Gardens* and I said so. Gale laughed. It was a host's laugh, high and cut short like a cough.

"Let me have your coat," he said. "Barbara's in the den. She'll be right up."

I shrugged off my parka and watched Gale hang it at the far end of the closet, away from his and Barbara's coats. Then Barbara came up some stairs near the dining room and walked stiff-legged down the hall toward me, her face tight like she was afraid something bad was going to happen. "Hello," I said. Then, before she could say anything, I leaned over and gave her a peck on the cheek.

I glanced at Gale to see if he'd minded. If he had, he didn't show it. I didn't look at Barbara to see what she thought.

"Well, how was your trip?" Barbara said. She spoke like she had to force the words out, like they hurt her throat.

"It was good," I said. "Good as could be. Under the circumstances." Somehow the word *circumstances* made me look away from her. "I like your house," I added quickly. "I didn't think they had houses like this out in the middle of Wyoming."

Gale smiled. "The company takes good care of their people. They may make us live out here with the jackrabbits, but they provide us with good housing."

"That's good," I said. Then we all just stood there a moment. Finally Barbara said, "Gale, don't you think we ought to let Alec freshen up before dinner?" Then she turned to me, only she didn't look right at me. "Come on. I'll show you to your room."

"And I'll get us something to drink. What would you like?" Gale said, putting his fingers together the way servants do in movies.

"Nothing for me," I answered. "Thanks anyway. You go ahead."

Barbara looked at me, squinting just a little, like she was sizing me up. "Your room's just up the hall," she said, and led the way. I followed her, noticing how she'd spread out over the past six years. She'd always been a bit hippy, but now she was big. Still, I must admit I didn't mind watching her walk.

At the end of the hallway, she opened a door and switched on the light. "This is your room," she said.

I looked in and saw pale blue wallpaper and a bed with a wheat-colored comforter and dust ruffle. There was a reading light on the headboard, and it made me remember how Chuck used to lay in bed at night reading Hardy Boys books. "Was this—" I started.

"This is the guest room," Barbara said quickly. She nodded toward a door just up the hall. "That was his room." Then she looked at me, her face hard. "I don't want you in there," she said. "I don't want anyone in there. Do you understand?"

I didn't say anything. Then she continued, "I've put some towels on the dresser for you. The bathroom's right next door. If there's anything else you—"

"It's good to see you again, Barbara," I interrupted. "I only wish to God there was another reason for it."

She looked at me. "Don't think you're fooling anybody with your 'Nothing for me, thanks,'" she said. "I smelled that Binaca on your breath. I know you've been drinking. Now, I don't mind you coming in here and invading our home, but I don't want you getting drunk and embarrassing us at the funeral. If you can't stay sober out of consideration for me and Gale, I hope you can do it for Chuck. Is that clear?"

I set my bag inside the door. "I'm still crazy about you too," I said. For a second, Barbara looked like she was going to slap me, but then she just turned and strode off down the hall.

"I loved him as much as you did," I called after her.

During dinner, Barbara barely looked at me, and she didn't say anything to either of us, except when she asked Gale to pass the roast or the potatoes. As soon as we finished eating, she excused herself, saying she had a headache, and went to bed. Gale apologized for her. "This has been awfully hard on her," he said. I didn't know whether "this" meant Chuck, or me.

Later that night, Gale and I were watching TV in the den. Gale was on his fourth Scotch, but I still hadn't had anything but club soda. I was worried I'd get the shakes, like I did at Intercept, but I didn't want to drink in front of Gale. I wanted him to think that Barbara had exaggerated about me, maybe even made some of it up.

Gale was talking about the TV. The oil company had paid for cable TV hook-ups; that's why he could get so many channels. Twenty-three in all. "Imagine that," he said, "twenty-three channels right here in the middle of nowhere." He gestured toward the walls with his drink, like nowhere was everywhere around us.

"That's something," I said. On the TV a young blonde was stepping out of one of those antique clawfooted bathtubs and wrapping a white towel around herself. There were tiny soapbubbles on her shoulders and thighs. From the music, I could tell she was going to get murdered soon.

"There's still nothing to watch, though," Gale said, and he took off his glasses and rubbed his eyes with the heels of his hands.

"You tired?" I said. "Don't let me keep you up if you are." I was hoping he'd call it a night so I could sneak myself some bourbon. I knew I wouldn't be able to sleep unless I had at least a couple of drinks—the last two nights I'd had to drink the better part of a fifth before I could even close my eyes.

"No, I'm not tired," he said. "How about you?"

"I'm fine," I said.

Gale nodded like he was glad I was fine, then walked over to the bar and poured himself another drink. I was thinking about Barbara's luck with men. For someone who hated drinking so much, she'd picked a couple of winners.

"He was on his way to see his girlfriend," Gale said then. "Tammy Winthrop. When they found him, they called me at the camp. Told me there'd been an accident. That's all they said." He came back over to the easy chair and sat down heavily. A little of the Scotch spilled on his cardigan sweater but he didn't seem to notice. He set his drink down on the endtable and sighed. "Hardest thing I ever had to do was identify him." He leaned forward and looked at me. "I mean, I thought they'd have him cleaned up and everything. But they didn't. They hadn't done a thing to him. All the blood and everything—" He stopped and sat back, shaking his head.

I was getting angry at him. I didn't want him to tell me this. But all I said was, "I'm sorry."

Gale sat forward in his chair again. "You had him when he was a boy. I'll always envy you that. But I saw him grow into a man. And

117

he was a fine man. He would've made one hell of a fine officer, I can tell you that." Then he started to cry. He covered his face with his hands and his shoulders heaved.

I couldn't think of anything to say, so I just sat there, looking at the TV. A man in a ski mask had stalked the blonde to her bedroom and she was crouching in the corner of her closet, trembling. The man had a barber's razor in his gloved hand, and the music was going crazy. I watched for a minute, then turned away. I wasn't scared—that kind of movie never scares me much—but I kept thinking about that girl's father watching the movie and seeing her crouched there like that, naked and afraid. Even though I knew it was all fake, I couldn't bear to watch it anymore.

I had to say something to Gale. "Are you all right?" I finally said.

"I'm sorry," Gale answered, and wiped his eyes with his handkerchief. "Please forgive me."

"There's nothing to forgive," I said. "I feel the same way you do."

Then Gale finished his drink and stood up. "Well, I guess it's about that time," he said, looking at his watch. "We'll have to get up early tomorrow." And then his face fell apart again.

"It'll be all right," I said, but I didn't get up, pat him on the shoulder, or anything like that.

"Yeah," he said, getting ahold of himself. "I guess it will." He shook his head. "Sorry."

"No problem," I said. "I understand."

"Well, goodnight then," he said, and started toward the door. But before he got there, he stopped and said, "Listen, Alec, if you're going to stay up awhile, why don't you go ahead and help yourself to anything you want?" And he waved his hand toward the bar.

I sat there, looking at him.

"I just want you to know I understand," he added. "And I'm sure Chuck would understand too."

I said, "Thanks, Gale. I appreciate that." But I decided that minute not to take a drop of liquor as long as I was in his house. And I wouldn't do it for him or Barbara or even myself; I'd do it for Chuck.

"I hope she's asleep," Gale said then.

"I do too," I answered.

He nodded, said goodnight again, and left.

I waited until I heard him climbing the stairs, then I got up and turned off the TV.

A few hours later, when I went up to my room, I stopped in the hallway outside Chuck's door and thought about opening it. I wasn't thinking about going in or anything—I just wanted to take a look. I wanted to see what his life had been like since he and Barbara left me. But I just stood there in the dim glow of the bathroom's night light and stared at the whorled pattern of the woodgrain. Then I went to bed.

I couldn't sleep, so I laid there awake. The longer I laid there, the more I started to wish I'd drunk some of Gale's liquor after all. But I couldn't take a drink, not until the funeral was over. Even if I had to stay awake all night, even if I had to get the shakes, I wasn't going to drink anything. I wanted to show Chuck I could do it; I wanted to prove to him I wasn't a drunk or a bad father.

So I laid there, trying not to think about drinking or Chuck. I thought about Betty and my new job at the Swift plant, and I wondered how long it'd be before I lost both. But thinking about Betty and my job only made me think of Barbara and the fights we had the winter I was laid off. I saw Chuck sitting on the old flowered couch, watching TV, pretending he didn't hear us fighting, and I remembered how I turned on him and shouted, "Don't just sit there like you're deaf and dumb" and how he swallowed like he was afraid I'd hit him and said, "Okay, Dad." And I remembered my lie about Mount Rainier again, I saw Chuck's lips trembling as he looked down at his boots and tried not to cry, and I felt like something inside me was falling off that cliff with the pebble he flicked over the edge. Then I tried to think about something else, it didn't matter what. I made myself remember my home town, the neighborhood I grew up in, and who lived in each of the houses on our street. I went down the block: the white two-story with the wraparound porch was the Petersons'; the squat brick house was the Randalls'; the rust-brown house was Old Man Roenicke's. But I couldn't remember who lived in the stucco house at the end of the block. Somehow it seemed so important that I remember. But there was nothing. The whole family was gone, as if it had never existed.

I made myself think of something else. I tried to remember all the houses and apartments I'd lived in since I was a boy and their addresses and phone numbers. I tried to remember the names of my classmates in high school and some of the dates I learned back in history class. But it was no use. Everything kept getting confused in my mind—places, addresses, numbers, names. I sat up and put my head in my hands.

Then I remembered Sheila, the red-haired waitress I was seeing when I first met Barbara. I hadn't thought of her in years. If I'd married her, everything would've been different. We would've been living somewhere far away, maybe on a farm, a quiet place in the country, and we'd probably have a child, a daughter maybe, a tomboy just starting to wear dresses. She would be slim and freckled, like Sheila, and when she laughed she'd toss her head back and hold her sides. Sheila and I would sit on the porch steps and watch her do cartwheels on the lawn. We'd be happy, nothing bad would have happened. Chuck would not even have been born.

I stood up then. I couldn't lay there anymore; I had to have a drink. I'd only have one, or at the most two—just enough to help me sleep. If I didn't get some sleep, I'd be worse at the funeral. And if I didn't drink something soon, I'd get the shakes.

But as I crept down the dark hallway, I heard something that stopped me. At first, I thought it was Barbara and Gale whispering, then I was sure it was the sound of them making love. I could've sworn I heard the small gasp Barbara used to make when I entered her. I'd forgotten that sound, and it cut through me like a cold wind. I stood outside their door and strained to hear. After a moment, I heard the sound again, and this time I knew what it was. It was Barbara, trying to cry quietly, so she wouldn't wake Gale.

I leaned my head against the wall then, and wondered if she had ever cried like that when I was sleeping beside her. And whether Chuck had ever stood outside our room in the dark, listening.

The next morning, when I went into the kitchen, Barbara was already there. She was wearing a yellow robe and drinking coffee from a blue enameled mug.

"Good morning," I said. I hadn't slept all night, and I felt worse than if I'd had a hangover.

"Gale's not up yet," she said, without looking at me. "I thought it best to let him sleep as long as he could."

I went to the counter and poured myself a cup of coffee. "That was good of you," I said. There was a Cuisinart on the counter next to the Mr. Coffee. I glanced at her fridge and stove. Harvest Gold.

I sat down at the table across from her. My head was throbbing and my eyes burned. I looked out the window. It was snowing, an easy snow, the kind that comes down peacefully and covers everything. The birdfeeder on the railing of the patio was already mounded over with snow. There weren't any birds around.

"Gale's a good man," I said. "I like him." I wasn't lying; I did like Gale, though I wished I didn't.

"I'd rather not talk right now," she said then, and pushed her fingers through her gray-blonde hair. "If there's something you'd like for breakfast, just go ahead and help yourself."

"I'm not hungry," I said.

She shrugged her shoulders. "Suit yourself."

Then we drank our coffee for a while without saying anything. Finally I put my cup down and said, "It's going to be a long day. It's going to be tough. Can't we be friends for just this one day?"

She didn't answer. She just sat there with her hands cradled around her cup for warmth.

"Damn it," I said. "I want to make this easier for you. Can't you see that?"

She kept looking at the coffee in her mug. "You could have made it easier for me by not coming," she said. "You've brought back a lot of bad memories."

I looked out the window, watched the snow drift down. "I haven't had a drink since yesterday afternoon."

"A half a day," she said.

"I know," I answered. "But it was rough. Especially last night. You don't know how bad I wanted a drink."

"Why?" she said then, tilting her head toward me. "So you wouldn't remember your son's name? So if someone said 'Chuck is dead' you'd just scratch your head and say 'Chuck who?'" She picked up her mug. Her hand was trembling.

"That's not fair," I said.

"What you did to Chuck and me wasn't fair either," she said back.

I dipped my spoon in my coffee and stirred it, though it was already cool.

"I wasn't myself," I said. "I was drinking too much."

She didn't say anything.

Then I said, "I heard you last night. I was walking down the hall and I heard you. It made me wonder if you ever laid awake crying like that when we were married."

She looked up from her coffee. "Don't make this day any harder than it has to be."

"I'm sorry," I said.

She picked up the coffee cup again. "Just remember that Gale invited you here, not me. If you had to come, you could have at least stayed at a motel."

"If I *had* to come?" I said. "Chuck is my *son*. I have just as much right to go to his funeral as you do."

"Maybe so," she said. "But what makes you think Chuck would want you at his funeral? Did you ever think that maybe he wouldn't have wanted you here any more than I do?"

I wanted to say that Chuck had never blamed me for any of it, that he always knew it was the booze, not me, that was responsible. I wanted to tell her that he had always loved me, despite everything she'd done to turn him against me. But I didn't say anything. I looked out the window and watched the evergreens grow slowly more white.

After a while, Barbara said, "I'm sorry. I was just trying to hurt you. I didn't mean it." She still had her hands cradled around her cup, though it must have been cold by now. "Can we please stop talking now?"

I nodded. "If you want."

Neither of us said anything after that until Gale came into the kitchen a few minutes later. He was wearing a navy blue robe and slippers. " 'Morning," he said. His face was splotchy and his eyes were red behind his thick glasses. I wondered if his head was hurting as much as mine.

"Are you all right?" I asked.

"I'm fine," he said, trying to smile. "How are you?"

"I'm fine, too," I said.

"Good. Good." Then he put his hands on Barbara's shoulders and leaned over and kissed the top of her head. "Did you sleep all right, dear?" he asked.

"Just fine," she said, looking at me.

At the funeral, Gale asked me to sit in the front pew with him and Barbara, but I said no and took a seat alone in the back of the church. I didn't listen to the minister's eulogy or sing any of the hymns. I just sat there and tried not to look at the flag-covered coffin, or at Barbara. I could hear her crying, that same quiet sobbing I'd heard the night before, but I wouldn't let myself look at her.

I didn't look at Chuck either. Even though I came all that way to see him, when we filed into the church past his open casket, I couldn't look at him. I bent over to look at him, but before I could see his face, my eyes closed. All I saw were the gold buttons of his dress blues and the white gloves on his crossed hands.

I didn't see him, but in a way I saw him wherever I looked. The small brick church was filled with his classmates from Officers' Training School, all wearing their dress blues too. They sat stiff, at attention, hands unmoving on their laps. It occurred to me then that it was just some strange accident that one of them was not my son. I could have sat beside any of their highchairs, feeding them applesauce. I could have helped any of them with their homework. I could have romped around the kitchen with any of them riding on my shoulders. But Chuck had been my son. Somehow, it seemed such a random thing.

It wasn't until after the funeral that I started to get the shakes. The snow had turned to sleet during the service and everyone was standing in the vestibule, bundling up before going outside. Barbara and Gale stood by the Crying Room, waiting for the funeral director to bring the limousine around. The members of Chuck's graduating class filed past them, shaking hands and saying how sorry they were to lose such a good friend and fellow officer. Barbara and Gale's friends comforted them too. The women cried and wiped their eyes with Kleenexes or handkerchiefs. Their husbands stood beside them, said a few words, then put on their hats like it was the only thing they could do to keep from crying themselves.

I turned away and looked outside. The cars were lining up in the parking lot, their lights already on. Their windshield wipers were barely keeping up with the sleet.

RAINIER

Just then, a tall, skinny girl with sand-colored hair came up to me and looked at my face, her forehead pursed. "You're Chuck's father, aren't you?" she asked.

"Yes," I said. "How did you know?" Barbara had introduced me to the minister and the funeral director as her former husband, but she hadn't mentioned anything about Chuck being my son, and I hadn't said anything. Gale had looked away, embarrassed, but he hadn't said anything either.

"I've seen pictures of you," she answered. I must have looked surprised because she added, "I'm Tammy. I was Chuck's girl-friend." Then she looked down at her folded hands. Her fingernails were bitten down and the skin around them was red and cracked. "He was on his way to see me when he had the accident," she said. "Sometimes I blame myself for it happening." Then her eyes began to swell with tears.

"I'm sorry," I started to say, but she took my arm suddenly.

"I want you to know," she said, "that Chuck forgave you before he died. He didn't hate you anymore. He even talked about the two of us driving up to Montana to see you, to set things right between you."

I couldn't believe what she was saying. "You're wrong," I said, pulling my arm away. "You're terribly wrong." I meant that Chuck had never hated me, that he'd always loved me in spite of every-thing, but Tammy didn't understand.

"No," she insisted. "It's true. He did forgive you." She took my arm again. "You have to believe that."

I stood there looking at her earnest face. For a second, it crossed my mind that I'd like to slap her. But I just said, "Thank you. I appreciate you telling me that."

"He really did love you," Tammy went on. "You have to re-member that."

I was beginning to feel dizzy, almost sick. "I'm sure he did," I said, and tried to smile. "He always said he did."

Tammy looked down a second. When she looked back up, her face was working. "Oh, Mr. Falk," she said, gulping back a sob, "I'm so sorry!" And then she gave me a quick hug and turned and hurried outside. I watched her run carefully down the slick sidewalk to a blue Oldsmobile waiting in the parking lot.

That was when the shaking started. It was almost as bad as that time at Intercept, when I couldn't lift my own fork or spoon and a nurse had to feed me like a baby. But it was a different kind of shaking, a scarier kind. I was shaking so much I thought I'd have to sit down right there on the floor. I put my hands in my pockets so no one could see them shake.

A minute later, Gale called across the vestibule to me. "It's time," he said, and nodded toward the limousine idling behind the hearse. But I couldn't move. I was trembling so bad I just stood there. Gale came over and said again that it was time to go.

"That's all right," I managed to say. "I'll catch a ride with someone else a little later."

"What are you talking about?" Gale said. "You don't even know anybody else here."

Barbara came over then. "What's wrong?" she asked. "Mr. Gilmer is waiting."

"Nothing's wrong," I said. "You two go on ahead. I'll catch up in a little while."

Barbara looked at me. "Are you all right?"

I couldn't look at her. "I'll be okay in a few minutes," I said. "I'll catch up with you then."

Gale put his hand on my arm. "I know how you feel," he said. "I'll ask Pastor Young if he can take you with him."

"Fine," I nodded. My teeth were chattering and I could hardly talk.

"Maybe you should sit down for a while," Barbara said.

"I'll do that," I answered. But I couldn't move.

RAINIER

"We've got to go," Gale said. "Are you sure you aren't coming with us?"

I nodded.

Gale took Barbara's arm then. "Come on, dear, everyone's waiting."

Barbara looked at me. "You won't try to go back to Bozeman before we get home, will you? I don't think you ought to drive right now. Not the way you're—" She didn't finish.

"I won't," I said.

Then she gave me her house key. "You can get a taxi to take you to the house," she said. "Maybe you can get some sleep. Or at least rest."

"You mean, maybe I can get a drink."

She looked like I had struck her. "No," she said, "I didn't mean that."

"You're sure you'll be all right?" Gale asked. I nodded yes. "Then we'd better go, dear," he said to Barbara.

The funeral director was standing beside the limousine under an umbrella, waiting to open the door for them. Barbara took a deep breath. "Okay," she said, still looking at me, then turned and went out into the sleet with Gale.

After the procession wound its way out of the church parking lot, I went out into the storm and began walking back to Barbara and Gale's house. I didn't know, then, why I wanted to walk instead of taking a taxi; after I reached the house I understood, but then, I just felt I had to do it, that somehow it would be wrong not to.

The house was on the other end of town, near the oil camp and the black pumping units rising out of the snow like giant grasshoppers, but Rose Creek was just a hospital, a post office, a community hall, a school, and a couple dozen blocks of stores and houses, so I didn't have far to walk. But it was awfully cold, and I didn't have any overshoes or gloves. After a few minutes, my hands and feet were numb, and the wind was blowing the sleet into my face so hard it stung. I felt exhausted, like I'd been walking for hours, even days. My breaths came out short and fast, little clouds the wind blew into nothing.

My shaking was getting worse. I had to have a drink, I couldn't wait any longer, so I walked as fast as I could. I walked past the silent houses with smoke rising from their chimneys, past the schoolyard where some children in snowmobile suits were playing King of the Hill on a mound of snow, past the turnoff that led to the highway where Chuck had died. I walked faster and faster until I was almost running. My face and hands burned from the cold, and I could tell without looking that they were white with frostbite.

When I finally reached the house, I stood on the front steps, the sleet pelting my back, and tried to open the door, but my hand was shaking so bad I couldn't get the key into the lock. I stood there a moment, trying to get ahold of myself. But it was no use. I couldn't even breathe right—I had to strain for every breath, as if the air was too thin—and I felt so empty and dizzy I had to hold onto the doorframe to keep from falling.

And then I saw myself climbing Rainier, inching my way up the sheer cliff, a terrible weight on my back, and it wasn't a lie anymore, I had really done it. And I hung onto Barbara's door, bracing myself against the rising wind.

I remember sitting in Gale's easy chair, drinking his bourbon and staring out his window at the ice-laden trees, but I don't remember going to Chuck's room. I don't even remember thinking about going there. I just remember finding myself swaying drunk in front of his door. And I remember deciding, as soon as I realized where I was and what I was about to do, that it'd been a mistake to come, that I should never have left Bozeman. Standing there, I saw myself driving across that empty state under the huge black sky, driving away from Barbara and Gale and what was left of my son, heading home, toward Betty and lovemaking and sleep. And I turned to leave.

But I turned back. I couldn't leave, not yet. I stood there a second, then took a deep breath and opened the door.

I'm not sure what exactly I expected—maybe I thought his room would give him back to me, if only for a moment, let me be with him for that last minute before he drove off to the accident that waited for him—but whatever it was, I didn't get what I wanted. The room was just a room. The bed was just a bed, the desk just a desk. Even the shirts that hung in his closet were just shirts. I stood there awhile, looking at everything, then opened the top drawer of the desk: blank paper, some pens, a ruler, and a calculator. In one corner there were some pencil shavings. I picked them up and they fell apart in my hands.

I sat down at the desk then and put my hot face against the cool wood. It felt good against my cheek, and it made me think of when I was in grade school and the teacher wanted to find out who had done something wrong. She'd tell everyone to put their heads down on their desks and close their eyes, then raise their hands if they were the one. Closing my eyes, I remembered how I felt those times when I hadn't done anything, how I liked sitting there, innocent, imagining someone else's guilty hand rising into the air.

At first I thought the storm had woken me. Sleet was striking the window, sounding like flung pellets of rice. But then I heard Barbara, her voice wavering. "What are you doing in here?" I lifted my head from the desk and tried to see through the darkness. But I saw only a shadow, haloed by the hall light, and I heard it say, "Why did you have to come in *here*?" Then she flicked on the overhead light. I shielded my eyes. Through the bright blur, I saw Gale standing behind her in the hall, his coat still in his hand.

"I knew we shouldn't have stayed so long at Muriel's," he was saying. "I knew something would happen."

Barbara came toward me. "I asked you not to come in here," she said. She looked around and bit her quivering lip. "Why did you have to—" she started, but couldn't finish.

I realized then that I'd taken away her last comfort, that from now on when she came into this room I'd be here with him. "I'm sorry," I said, and stood up. My forehead swelled and throbbed, and I almost lost my balance.

"You're drunk," Barbara said then, and she stepped toward me, her hands clenched at her sides.

I wasn't drunk, not anymore, but it didn't matter. And it didn't matter that Barbara and Gale were angry at me. Nothing mattered now. It was all over. And suddenly I felt numb, almost peaceful, even though I knew it couldn't last, that any minute now all the pain and sorrow would come back, maybe even worse than before.

Barbara said something to me then, but I didn't hear. I just looked at her. Then I reached out and put my arms around her. She stayed stiff in my arms and kept her hands at her sides, but she didn't back away from me. I held her tight. "Chuck is dead," I told her. I said it like I'd only just found out about it and thought she ought to know.

Glossolalia

T HAT WINTER, like every winter before it, my father woke early each day and turned up the thermostat so the house would be warm by the time my mother and I got out of bed. Sometimes I'd hear the furnace kick in and the shower come on down the hall and I'd wake just long enough to be angry that he'd woken me. But usually I slept until my mother had finished making our breakfast. By then, my father was already at Goodyear, opening the service bay for the customers who had to drop their cars off before going to work themselves. Sitting in the sunny kitchen, warmed by the heat from the register and the smell of my mother's coffee, I never thought about him dressing in the cold dark or shoveling out the driveway by porchlight. If I thought of him at all, it was only to feel glad he was not there. In those days my father and I fought a lot, though probably not much more than most fathers and sons. I was sixteen then, a tough age. And he was forty, an age I've since learned is even tougher.

But that winter I was too concerned with my own problems to think about my father's. I was a skinny, unathletic, sorrowful boy who had few friends, and I was in love with Molly Rasmussen, one of the prettiest girls in Glencoe and the daughter of a man who had stopped my father on Main Street that fall, cursed him, and threatened to break his face. My father had bought a used Ford Galaxie from Mr. Rasmussen's lot, but he hadn't been able to make the payments and eventually Mr. Rasmussen repossessed it. Without a second car my mother couldn't get to work—she had taken a job at the school lunchroom, scooping out servings of mashed potatoes and green beans—so we drove our aging Chevy to Minneapolis, where no one knew my father, and bought a rust-pitted yellow Studebaker. A few days later Molly Rasmussen passed me in the hall at school and said, "I see you've got a new car," then laughed. I was so mortified I hurried into a rest room, locked myself in a stall, and stood there for several minutes, breathing hard. Even after the bell rang for the next class, I didn't move. I was furious at my father. I blamed him for the fact that Molly despised me, just as I had for some time blamed him for everything else that was wrong with my life—my gawky looks, my discount store clothes, my lack of friends.

That night, and others like it, I lay in bed and imagined who I'd be if my mother had married someone handsome and popular like Dick Moore, the PE teacher, or Smiley Swenson, who drove stock cars at the county fair, or even Mr. Rasmussen. Years before, my mother had told me how she met my father. A girl who worked with her at Woolworth's had asked her if she wanted to go out with a friend of her boyfriend's, an army man just back from the war. My mother had never agreed to a blind date before, or dated an older man, but for some reason this time she said yes. Lying there, I thought about that fateful moment. It seemed so fragile—she could as easily have said no and changed everything—and I wished, then, that she had said no, I wished she'd said she didn't date strangers or she already had a date or she was going out of town—anything to alter the chance conjunction that would eventually produce me.

I know now that there was something suicidal about my desire to undo my parentage, but then I knew only that I wanted to be someone else. And I blamed my father for that wish. If I'd had a different father, I reasoned, I would be better looking, happier, more popular. When I looked in the mirror and saw my father's thin face, his rust-red hair, downturned mouth, and bulging Adam's apple, I didn't know who I hated more, him or me. That winter I began parting my hair on the right instead of the left, as my father did, and whenever the house was empty I worked on changing my voice, practicing the inflections and accents of my classmates' fathers as if they were clues to a new life. I even practiced one's walk, another's crooked smile, a third's wink. I did not think, then, that my father knew how I felt about him, but now that I have a son of my own, a son almost as old as I was then, I know different.

If I had known what my father was going through that winter, maybe I wouldn't have treated him so badly. But I didn't know anything until the January morning of his breakdown. I woke that morning to the sound of voices downstairs in the kitchen. At first I thought the sound was the wind rasping in the bare branches of the cottonwood outside my window, then I thought it was the radio. But after I lay there a moment I recognized my parents' voices. I couldn't tell what they were saying, but I knew they were arguing. They'd been arguing more than usual lately, and I hated it—not so much because I wanted them to be happy, though I did, but because I knew they'd take their anger out on me, snapping at me, telling me to chew with my mouth closed, asking me who gave me permission to put my feet up on the coffee table, ordering me to clean my room. I buried one ear in my pillow and covered the other with my blankets, but I could still hear them. They sounded distant, yet somehow close, like the sea crashing in a shell held to the ear. But after a while I couldn't hear even the muffled sound of their voices, and I sat up in the bars of gray light slanting through the blinds and listened to the quiet. I didn't know what was worse:

their arguments or their silences. I sat there, barely breathing, waiting for some noise.

Finally I heard the back door bang shut and, a moment later, the Chevy cough to life. Only then did I dare get out of bed. Crossing to the window, I raised one slat of the blinds with a finger and saw, in the dim light, the driveway drifted shut with snow. Then my father came out of the garage and began shoveling, scooping the snow furiously and flinging it over his shoulder, as if each shovelful were a continuation of the argument. I couldn't see his face, but I knew that it was red and that he was probably cursing under his breath. As he shoveled, the wind scuffed the drifts around him, swirling the snow into his eyes, but he didn't stop or set his back to the wind. He just kept shoveling fiercely, and suddenly it occurred to me that he might have a heart attack, just as my friend Rob's father had the winter before. For an instant I saw him slump over his shovel, then collapse face-first into the snow. As soon as this thought came to me, I did my best to convince myself that it arose from love and terror, but even then I knew part of me wished his death, and that knowledge went through me like a chill.

I lowered the slat on the blinds and got back into bed. The house was quiet but not peaceful. I knew that somewhere in the silence my mother was crying and I thought about going to comfort her, but I didn't. After a while I heard my father rev the engine and back the Chevy down the driveway. Still I didn't get up. And when my mother finally came to tell me it was time to get ready, her eyes and nose red and puffy, I told her I wasn't feeling well and wanted to stay home. Normally she would have felt my forehead and cross-examined me about my symptoms, but that day I knew she'd be too upset to bother. "Okay, Danny," she said. "Call me if you think you need to see a doctor." And that was it. She shut the door and a few minutes later I heard the whine of the Studebaker's cold engine, and then she was gone.

GLOSSOLALIA

It wasn't long after my mother left that my father came home. I was lying on the couch in the living room, trying to figure out the hidden puzzle on "Concentration," when I heard a car pull into the driveway. At first I thought my mother had changed her mind and come back to take me to school. But then the back door sprang open and I heard him. It was a sound I had never heard before, and since have heard only in my dreams, a sound that will make me sit up in the thick dark, my eyes open to nothing and my breath panting. I don't know how to explain it, other than to say that it was a kind of crazy language, like speaking in tongues. It sounded as if he were crying and talking at the same time, and in some strange way his words had become half-sobs and his sobs something more than words—or words turned inside out, so that only their emotion and not their meaning came through. It scared me. I knew something terrible had happened, and I didn't know what to do. I wanted to go to him and ask what was wrong, but I didn't dare. I switched off the sound on the TV so he wouldn't know I was home and sat there staring at Hugh Downs' smiling face. But then I couldn't stand it anymore and I got up and ran down the hall to the kitchen. There, in the middle of the room, wearing his Goodyear jacket and workclothes, was my father. He was on his hands and knees, his head hanging as though it were too heavy to support, and he was rocking back and forth and babbling in a rhythmic stutter. It's funny, but the first thing I thought when I saw him like that was the way he used to give me rides on his back, when I was little, bucking and neighing like a horse. And as soon as I thought it, I felt my heart lurch in my chest. "Dad?" I said. "What's wrong?" But he didn't hear me. I went over to him then. "Dad?" I said again, and touched him on the shoulder. He jerked at the touch and looked up at me, his lips moving but no sounds coming out of them now. His forehead was knotted and his eyes were red, almost raw-looking. He swallowed hard and for the first time spoke words

I could recognize, though I did not understand them until years later, when I was myself a father.

"Danny," he said. "Save me."

Before I could finish dialing the school lunchroom's number, my mother pulled into the driveway. Looking out the window, I saw her jump out of the car and run up the slick sidewalk, her camel-colored overcoat open and flapping in the wind. For a moment I was confused. Had I already called her? How much time had passed since I found my father on the kitchen floor? A minute? An hour? Then I realized that someone else must have told her something was wrong.

She burst in the back door then and called out, "Bill? Bill? Are you here?"

"Mom," I said, "Dad's—" and then I didn't know how to finish the sentence.

She came in the kitchen without stopping to remove her galoshes. "Oh, Bill," she said when she saw us, "are you all right?"

My father was sitting at the kitchen table now, his hands fluttering in his lap. A few moments before, I had helped him to his feet and, draping his arm over my shoulders, led him to the table like a wounded man.

"Helen," he said. "It's you." He said it as if he hadn't seen her for years.

My mother went over and knelt beside him. "I'm so sorry," she said, but whether that statement was born of sorrow over something she had said or done or whether she just simply and guiltlessly wished he weren't suffering, I never knew. Taking his hands in hers, she added, "There's nothing to worry about. Everything's going to be fine." Then she turned to me. Her brown hair was wind-blown, and her face was so pale the smudges of rouge on her cheeks looked like bruises. "Danny, I want you to leave us alone for a few minutes."

I looked at her red-rimmed eyes and tight lips. "Okay," I said, and went back to the living room. There, I sat on the sagging couch and stared at the television, the contestants' mouths moving wordlessly, their laughs eerily silent. I could hear my parents talking, their steady murmur broken from time to time by my father sobbing and my mother saying "Bill" over and over, in the tone mothers use to calm their babies, but I couldn't hear enough of what they said to know what had happened. And I didn't want to know either. I wanted them to be as silent as the people on the TV, I wanted all the words to stop, all the crying.

I lay down and closed my eyes, trying to drive the picture of my father on the kitchen floor out of my head. My heart was beating so hard I could feel my pulse tick in my throat. I was worried about my father but I was also angry that he was acting so strange. It didn't seem fair that I had to have a father like that. I'd never seen anybody else's father act that way, not even in a movie.

Outside, the wind shook the evergreens and every now and then a gust would rattle the windowpane. I lay there a long time, listening to the wind, until my heart stopped beating so hard.

Some time later, my mother came into the room and sat on the edge of the chair under the sunburst mirror. Her forehead was creased, and there were black mascara streaks on her cheeks. Leaning toward me, her hands clasped, she asked me how I was feeling.

"What do you mean?" I asked. I didn't know if she was asking whether I still felt sick or if she meant something else.

She bit her lip. "I just wanted to tell you not to worry," she said. "Everything's going to be all right." Her breath snagged on the last word, and I could hear her swallowing.

"What's wrong?" I asked.

She opened her mouth as if she were about to answer, but suddenly her eyes began to tear. "We'll talk about it later," she said. "After the doctor's come. Just don't worry, okay? I'll explain everything."

"The doctor?" I said.

"I'll explain later," she answered.

Then she left and I didn't hear anything more until ten or fifteen minutes had passed and the doorbell rang. My mother ran to the door and opened it, and I heard her say, "Thank you for coming so quickly. He's in the kitchen." As they hurried down the hall past the living room, I caught a glimpse of Dr. Lewis and his black leather bag. It had been years since the doctors in our town, small as it was, made house calls, so I knew now that my father's problem was something truly serious. The word *emergency* came into my mind, and though I tried to push it out, it kept coming back.

For the next half-hour or so, I stayed in the living room, listening to the droning sound of Dr. Lewis and my parents talking. I still didn't know what had happened or why. All I knew was that my father was somebody else now, somebody I didn't know. I tried to reconcile the man who used to read to me at night when my mother was too tired, the man who patiently taught me how to measure and cut plywood for a birdhouse, even the man whose cheeks twitched when he was angry at me and whose silences were suffocating, with the man I had just seen crouched like an animal on the kitchen floor babbling some incomprehensible language. But I couldn't. And though I felt sorry for him and his suffering, I felt as much shame as sympathy. *This is your father*, I told myself. *This is you when you're older.*

It wasn't until after Dr. Lewis had left and my father had taken the tranquilizers and gone upstairs to bed that my mother came back into the living room, sat down on the couch beside me, and told me what had happened. "Your father," she began, and her voice cracked. Then she controlled herself and said, "Your father has been fired from his job."

I looked at her. "Is that it?" I said. "That's what all this fuss is about?" I couldn't believe he'd put us through all this for something so unimportant. All he had to do was get a new job. What was the big deal?

"Let me explain," my mother said. "He was fired some time ago. Ten days ago, to be exact. But he hadn't said anything to me about it, and he just kept on getting up and going down to work every morning, like nothing had happened. And every day Mr. Siverhus told him to leave, and after arguing a while, he'd go. Then he'd spend the rest of the day driving around until quitting time, when he'd finally come home. But Mr. Siverhus got fed up and changed the locks, and when your father came to work today he couldn't get in. He tried all three entrances, and when he found his key didn't work in any of them, well, he threw a trash barrel through the showroom window and went inside."

She paused for a moment, I think to see how I was taking this. I was trying to picture my father throwing a barrel through that huge, expensive window. It wasn't easy to imagine. Even at his most angry, he had never been violent. He had never even threatened to hit me or my mother. But now he'd broken a window, and the law.

My mother went on. "Then when he was inside, he found that Mr. Siverhus had changed the lock on his office too, so he kicked the door in. When Mr. Siverhus came to work, he found your dad sitting at his desk, going over service accounts." Her lips started to tremble. "He could have called the police," she said, "but he called me instead. We owe him for that."

That's the story my mother told me. Though I was to find out later that she hadn't told me the entire truth, she had told me enough of it to make me realize that my father had gone crazy. Something in him—whatever slender idea or feeling it is that connects us to the world—had broken, and he was not in the world anymore, he was outside it, horribly outside it, and could not get back in no matter how he tried. Somehow I knew this, even then. And I wondered if someday the same thing would happen to me.

The rest of that day, I stayed downstairs, watching TV or reading *Sports Illustrated* or *Life*, while my father slept or rested. My mother sat beside his bed, reading her ladies magazines while he slept and talking to him whenever he woke, and every now and then she came downstairs to tell me he was doing fine. She spoke as if he had some temporary fever, some twenty-four-hour virus, that would be gone by morning.

But the next morning, a Saturday, my father was still not himself. He didn't feel like coming down for breakfast, so she made him scrambled eggs, sausage, and toast and took it up to him on a tray. He hadn't eaten since the previous morning, but when she came back down awhile later all the food was still on the tray. She didn't say anything about the untouched meal; she just said my father wanted to talk to me.

"I can't, " I said. "I'm eating." I had one sausage patty and a few bites of scrambled egg left on my plate.

"Not this minute," she said. "When you're done."

I looked out the window. It had been snowing all morning, and the evergreens in the backyard looked like flocked Christmas trees waiting for strings of colored lights. Some sparrows were flying in and out of the branches, chirping, and others were lined up on the crossbars of the clothesline poles, their feathers fluffed out and blowing in the wind.

"I'm supposed to meet Rob at his house," I lied. "I'll be late."

"Danny," she said, in a way that warned me not to make her say any more.

"All right," I said, and I shoved my plate aside and got up. "But I don't have much time."

Upstairs, I stopped at my father's closed door. Normally I would have walked right in, but that day I felt I should knock. I felt as if I were visiting a stranger. Even his room—I didn't think of it as belonging to my mother anymore—seemed strange, somehow separate from the rest of the house.

When I knocked, my father said, "Is that you, Danny?" and I stepped inside. All the blinds were shut, and the dim air smelled like a thick, musty mixture of hair tonic and Aqua Velva. My father was sitting on the edge of his unmade bed, wearing his old brown robe, nubbled from years of washings, and maroon corduroy slippers. His face was blotchy, and his eyes were dark and pouched.

"Mom said you wanted to talk to me," I said.

He touched a spot next to him on the bed. "Here. Sit down."

I didn't move. "I've got to go to Rob's," I said.

He cleared his throat and looked away. For a moment we were silent, and I could hear the heat register ticking.

"I just wanted to tell you to take good care of your mother," he said then.

I shifted my weight from one foot to the other. "What do you mean?"

He looked back at me, his gaze steady and empty, and I wondered how much of the way he was that moment was his medication and how much himself. "She needs someone to take care of her," he said. "That's all."

"What about you? Aren't you going to take care of her anymore?"

He cleared his throat again. "If I can."

"I don't get it," I said. "Why are you doing this to us? What's going on?"

"Nothing's going on," he answered. "That's the problem. Not a thing is going on."

"I don't know what you mean. I don't like it when you say things I can't understand."

"I don't like it either," he said. Then: "That wasn't me yesterday. I want you to know that."

"It sure looked like you. If it wasn't you, who was it then?"

He stood up and walked across the carpet to the window. But he didn't open the blinds; he just stood there, his back to me. "It's all right for you to be mad," he said.

"I'm not mad."

141

"Don't lie, Danny."

"I'm not lying. I just like my father to use the English language when he talks to me, that's all."

For a long moment he was quiet. It seemed almost as if he'd forgotten I was in the room. Then he said, "My grandmother used to tell me there were exactly as many stars in the sky as there were people. If someone was born, there'd be a new star in the sky that night, and you could find it if you looked hard enough. And if someone died, you'd see that person's star fall."

"What are you talking about?" I said.

"People," he answered. "Stars."

Then he just stood there, staring at the blinds. I wondered if he was seeing stars there, or his grandmother, or what. And all of a sudden I felt my throat close up and my eyes start to sting. I was surprised—a moment before I'd been so angry, but now I was almost crying.

I tried to swallow, but I couldn't. I wanted to know what was wrong, so I could know how to feel about it; I wanted to be sad or angry, either one, but not both at the same time. "What *happened*?" I finally said. "*Tell* me."

He turned, but I wasn't sure he'd heard me, because he didn't answer for a long time. And when he did, he seemed to be answering some other question, one I hadn't asked.

"I was so arrogant," he said. "I thought my life would work out."

I stood there looking at him. "I don't understand."

"I hope you never do," he said. "I hope to God you never do."

"Quit talking like that."

"Like what?"

"Like you're so *smart* and everything. Like you're above all of this when it's you that's causing it all."

He looked down at the floor and shook his head slowly.

"Well?" I said. "Aren't you going to say something?"

GLOSSOLALIA

He looked up. "You're a good boy, Danny. I'm proud of you. I wish I could be a better father for you."

I hesitate now to say what I said next. But then I didn't hesitate.

"So do I," I said bitterly. "So the hell do I." And I turned to leave.

"Danny, wait," my father said.

But I didn't wait. And when I shut the door, I shut it hard.

Two days later, after he took to fits of weeping and laughing, we drove my father to the VA hospital in Minneapolis. Dr. Lewis had already called the hospital and made arrangements for his admission, so we were quickly escorted to his room on the seventh floor, where the psychiatric patients were kept. I had expected the psych ward to be a dreary, prisonlike place with barred doors and gray, windowless walls, but if anything, it was cheerier than the rest of the hospital. There were sky blue walls in the hallway, hung here and there with watercolor landscapes the patients had painted, and sunny yellow walls in the rooms, and there was a brightly lit lounge with a TV, card tables, and a shelf full of board games, and even a crafts center where the patients could do decoupage, leatherwork, mosaics, and macrame. And the patients we saw looked so normal that I almost wondered whether we were in the right place. Most of them were older, probably veterans of the First World War, but a few were my father's age or younger. The old ones were the friendliest, nodding their bald heads or waving their liver-spotted hands as we passed, but even those who only looked at us seemed pleasant or, at the least, not hostile.

I was relieved by what I saw but evidently my father was not, for his eyes still had the quicksilver shimmer of fear they'd had all during the drive from Glencoe. He sat stiffly in the wheelchair and looked at the floor passing between his feet as the big-boned nurse pushed him down the hall toward his room.

We were lucky, the nurse told us, chatting away in a strange accent, which I later learned was Czech. There had been only one private room left, and my father had gotten it. And it had a *lovely* view of the hospital grounds. Sometimes she herself would stand in front of that window and watch the snow fall on the birches and park benches. It was such a beautiful sight. She asked my father if that didn't sound nice, but he didn't answer.

Then she wheeled him into the room and parked the chair beside the white, starched-looking bed. My father hadn't wanted to sit in the chair when we checked him in at the admissions desk, but now he didn't show any desire to get out of it.

"Well, what do you think of your room, Mr. Conroy?" the nurse asked. My mother stood beside her, a handkerchief squeezed in her hand.

My father looked at the chrome railing on the bed, the stainless steel tray beside it, and the plastic-sealed water glasses on the tray. Then he looked at my mother and me.

"I suppose it's where I should be," he said.

During the five weeks my father was in the hospital, my mother drove to Minneapolis twice a week to visit him. Despite her urgings, I refused to go with her. I wanted to forget about my father, to erase him from my life. But I didn't tell her that. I told her I couldn't stand to see him in that awful place, and she felt sorry for me and let me stay home. But almost every time she came back, she'd have a gift for me from him: a postcard of Minnehaha Falls decoupaged onto a walnut plaque, a leather billfold with my initials burned into the cover, a belt decorated with turquoise and white beads. And a request: would I come see him that weekend? But I never went.

Glencoe was a small town, and like all small towns it was devoted to gossip. I knew my classmates had heard about my father —many of them had no doubt driven past Goodyear to see the broken window the way they'd drive past a body shop to see a car that had been totaled—but only Rob said anything. When he asked what had happened, I told him what Dr. Lewis had told me, that my father was just overworked and exhausted. He didn't believe me any more than I believed Dr. Lewis, but he pretended to accept that explanation. I wasn't sure if I liked him more for that pretense, or less.

It took a couple of weeks for the gossip to reach me. One day during lunch Rob told me that Todd Knutson, whose father was a mechanic at Goodyear, was telling everybody my father had been fired for embezzling. "I know it's a dirty lie," Rob said, "but some kids think he's telling the truth, so you'd better do something."

"Like what?" I said.

"Tell them the truth. Set the record straight."

I looked at my friend's earnest, acne-scarred face. As soon as he'd told me the rumor, I'd known it was true, and in my heart I had already convicted my father. But I didn't want my best friend to know that. Perhaps I was worried that he would turn against me too and I'd be completely alone.

"You bet I will," I said. "I'll make him eat those words."

But I had no intention of defending my father. I was already planning to go see Mr. Siverhus right after school and ask him, straight out, for the truth, so I could confront my father with the evidence and shame him the way he had shamed me. I was furious with him for making me even more of an outcast than I had been—I was the son of a *criminal* now—and I wanted to make him pay for it. All during my afternoon classes, I imagined going to see him at the hospital and telling him I knew his secret. He'd deny it at first, I was sure, but as soon as he saw I knew everything, he'd confess. He'd beg my forgiveness, swearing he'd never do anything to embarrass me or my mother again, but nothing he could say would make any difference—I'd just turn and walk away. And if I were called into court to testify against him, I'd take the stand and swear to tell the whole truth and nothing but the truth, my eyes steady on him all the while, watching him sit there beside his lawyer, his head hung, speechless.

I was angry at my mother too, because she hadn't told me everything. But I didn't realize until that afternoon, when I drove down to Goodyear to see Mr. Siverhus, just how much she hadn't told me.

Mr. Siverhus was a tall, silver-haired man who looked more like a banker than the manager of a tire store. He was wearing a starched white shirt, a blue-and-gray striped tie with a silver tie tack, and iridescent sharkskin trousers, and when he shook my hand he smiled so hard his crow's-feet almost hid his eyes. He led me into his small but meticulous office, closing the door on the smell of grease and the noise of impact wrenches removing lugs from wheels, and I blurted out my question before either of us even sat down.

"Who told you that?" he asked.

"My mother," I answered. I figured he wouldn't lie to me if he thought my mother had already told me the truth. Then I asked him again: "Is it true?"

Mr. Siverhus didn't answer right away. Instead, he gestured toward a chair opposite his gray metal desk and waited until I sat in it. Then he pushed some carefully stacked papers aside, sat on the edge of the desk, and asked me how my father was doing. I didn't really know—my mother kept saying he was getting better, but I wasn't sure I could believe her. Still, I said, "Fine."

He nodded. "I'm glad to hear that," he said. "I'm really terribly sorry about everything that's happened. I hope you and your mother know that."

He wanted me to say something, but I didn't. Standing up, he wandered over to the gray file cabinet and looked out the window at the showroom, where the new tires and batteries were on display. He sighed, and I knew he didn't want to be having this conversation.

"What your mother told you is true," he said then. "Bill was taking money. Not much, you understand, but enough that it soon became obvious we had a problem. After some investigating, we found out he was the one. I couldn't have been more surprised. Your father had been a loyal and hardworking employee for years—we never would have put him in charge of the service department otherwise—and he was the last person I would've expected to be stealing from us. But when we confronted him with it, he admitted it. He'd been having trouble making his mortgage payments, he said, and in a weak moment he'd taken some money and, later on, a little more. He seemed genuinely sorry about it and he swore he'd pay back every cent, so we gave him another chance."

"But he did it again, didn't he?" I said.

I don't know if Mr. Siverhus noticed the anger shaking my voice or not. He just looked at me and let out a slow breath. "Yes," he said sadly. "He did. And so I had to fire him. I told him we wouldn't prosecute if he returned the money, and he promised he would."

Then he went behind his desk and sat down heavily in his chair. "I hope you understand."

"I'm not blaming you," I said. "You didn't do anything wrong."

He leaned over the desk toward me. "I appreciate that," he said. "You don't know how badly I've felt about all of this. I keep thinking that maybe I should have handled it differently. I don't know, when I think that he might have taken his life because of this, well, I—"

"Taken his life?" I interrupted.

Mr. Siverhus sat back in his chair. "Your mother didn't tell you?"

I shook my head and closed my eyes for a second. I felt as if

147

something had broken loose in my chest and risen into my throat, making it hard to breathe, to think.

"I assumed you knew," he said. "I'm sorry, I shouldn't have said anything."

"Tell me," I said.

"I think you'd better talk to your mother about this, Danny. I don't think I should be the one to tell you."

"I need to know," I said.

Mr. Siverhus looked at me for a long moment. Then he said, "Very well. But you have to realize that your father was under a lot of stress. I'm sure that by the time he gets out of the hospital, he'll be back to normal, and you won't ever have to worry about him getting like that again."

I nodded. I didn't believe him, but I wanted him to go on.

Mr. Siverhus took a deep breath and let it out slowly. "When I came to work that morning and found your father in his office, he had a gun in his hand. A revolver. At first, I thought he was going to shoot me. But then he put it up to his own head. I tell you, I was scared. 'Bill,' I said, 'that's not the answer.' And then I just kept talking. It took me ten or fifteen minutes to get him to put the gun down. Then he left, and that's when I called your mother."

I must have had a strange look on my face because the next thing he said was, "Are you all right?"

I nodded, but I wasn't all right. I felt woozy, as if I'd just discovered another world inside this one, a world that made this one false. I wanted to leave, but I wasn't sure I could stand up. Then I did.

"Thank you, Mr. Siverhus," I said, and reached out to shake his hand. I wanted to say more but there was nothing to say. I turned and left.

Outside in the parking lot, I stood beside the Chevy, looking at the new showroom window and breathing in the cold. I was thinking how, only a few months before, I had been looking through my father's dresser for his old army uniform, which I wanted to wear to Rob's Halloween party, and I'd found the revolver tucked under his dress khakis in the bottom drawer. My father had always been full of warnings—don't mow the lawn barefoot, never go swimming in a river, always drive defensively—but he had never even mentioned he owned this gun, much less warned me not to touch it. I wondered why, and I held the gun up to the light, as if I could somehow see through it to an understanding of its meaning. But I couldn't—or at least I refused to believe that I could—and I put it back exactly where I found it and never mentioned it to anyone.

Now, standing there in the bitter cold, I saw my father sitting at a desk that was no longer his and holding that same gun to his head. And I realized that if he had killed himself with it, the police would have found my fingerprints on its black handle.

I didn't tell my mother what I had learned from Mr. Siverhus, and I didn't tell anyone else either. After dinner that night I went straight to my room and stayed there. I wanted to be alone, to figure things out, but the more I thought, the more I didn't know what to think. I wondered if it was starting already, if I was already going crazy like my father, because I wasn't sure who I was or what I felt. It had been a long time since I'd prayed, but that night I prayed that when I woke the next day everything would make sense again.

But the next morning I was still in a daze. Everything seemed so false, so disconnected from the real world I had glimpsed the day before, that I felt disoriented, almost dizzy. At school, the chatter of my classmates sounded as meaningless as my father's babble, and everything I saw seemed out of focus, distorted, the way things do just before you faint. Walking down the hall, I saw Todd Knutson standing by his locker, talking with Bonnie Zempel, a friend of Molly Rasmussen's, and suddenly I found myself walking up to them. I didn't know what I was going to say or do, I hadn't planned anything, and when I shoved Todd against his locker, it surprised me as much as it did him.

149

"I hope you're happy now," I said to him. "My father *died* last night." I'm not sure I can explain it now, but in a way I believed what I was saying, and my voice shook with a genuine grief.

Todd slowly lowered his fists. "What?" he said, and looked quickly at Bonnie's startled, open face.

"He had *cancer*," I said, biting down on the word to keep my mind from whirling. "A tumor on his brain. That's why he did the things he did, taking that money and breaking that window and everything. He couldn't help it."

And then my grief was too much for me, and I turned and strode down the hall, tears coming into my eyes. I waited until I was around the corner and out of their sight, then I started running, as fast as I could. Only then did I come back into the world and wonder what I had done.

That afternoon, my mother appeared at the door of my algebra class in her blue uniform and black hair net. At first I thought she was going to embarrass me by waving at me, as she often did when she happened to pass one of my classrooms, but then I saw the look on her face. "Excuse me, Mr. Laughlin," she said grimly, "I'm sorry to interrupt your class but I need to speak with my son for a moment."

Mr. Laughlin turned his dour face from the blackboard, his stick of chalk suspended in mid-calculation, and said, "Certainly, Mrs. Conroy. I hope there's nothing the matter."

"No," she said. "It's nothing to worry about."

But out in the hall, she slapped my face hard.

"How *dare* you say your father is dead," she said through clenched teeth. Her gray eyes were flinty and narrow.

"I didn't," I answered.

She raised her hand and slapped me again, even harder this time.

"Don't you lie to me, Daniel."

I started to cry. "Well, I wish he *was*," I said. "I wish he was dead, so all of this could be over."

My mother raised her hand again, but then she let it fall. "Go," she said. "Get away from me. I can't bear to look at you another minute."

I went back into the classroom and sat down. I felt awful about hurting my mother, but not so awful that I wasn't worried whether my classmates had heard her slap me or noticed my burning cheek. I saw them looking at me and shaking their heads, heard them whispering and laughing under their breath, and I stood up, my head roiling, and asked if I could be excused.

Mr. Laughlin looked at me. Then, without even asking what was wrong, he wrote out a pass to the nurse's office and handed it to me. As I left the room, I heard him say to the class, "That's enough. If I hear one more remark . . ."

Later, lying on a cot in the nurse's office, my hands folded over my chest, I closed my eyes and imagined I was dead and my parents and classmates were kneeling before my open coffin, their heads bowed in mourning.

After that day, my mother scheduled meetings for me with Father Ondahl, our priest, and Mr. Jenseth, the school counselor. She said she hoped they could help me through this difficult time, then added, "Obviously, I can't." I saw Father Ondahl two or three times, and as soon as I assured him that I still had my faith, though I did not, he said I'd be better off just seeing Mr. Jenseth from then on. I saw Mr. Jenseth three times a week for the next month, then once a week for the rest of the school year. I'm not sure how those meetings helped, or even if they did. All I know is that, in time, my feelings about my father, and about myself, changed.

My mother continued her visits to my father, but she no longer asked me to go along with her, and when she came home from seeing him, she waited until I asked before she'd tell me how he was. I wondered whether she'd told him I was seeing a counselor, and why, but I didn't dare ask. And I wondered if she'd ever forgive me for my terrible lie.

Then one day, without telling me beforehand, she returned from Minneapolis with my father. "Danny," she called, and I came out of the living room and saw them in the entryway. My father was stamping the snow off his black wingtips, and he had a suitcase in one hand and a watercolor of our house in the other, the windows yellow with light and a thin swirl of gray smoke rising from the red brick chimney. He looked pale and even thinner than I remembered. I was so surprised to see him, all I could say was, "You're home."

"That's right," he said, and put down the suitcase and painting. "The old man's back." Then he tried to smile, but it came out more like a wince. I knew he wanted me to hug him and say how happy I was to see him, and part of me wanted to do that, too. But I didn't. I just shook his hand as I would have an uncle's or a stranger's, then picked up the painting and looked at it.

"This is nice," I said. "Real nice."

"I'm glad you like it," he answered.

And then we just stood there until my mother said, "Well, let's get you unpacked, dear, and then we can all sit down and talk."

Despite everything that had happened, our life together after that winter was relatively peaceful. My father got a job at Firestone, and though for years he barely made enough to meet expenses, eventually he worked his way up to assistant manager and earned a good living. He occasionally lost his temper and succumbed to self-pity as he always had, but for the rest of his life, he was as normal and sane as anybody. Perhaps Dr. Lewis had been right after all, and all my father had needed was a good rest. In any case, by the time I was grown and married myself, his breakdown seemed a strange and impossible dream and I wondered, as I watched him play with my infant son, if I hadn't imagined some of it. It amazed me that a life could break so utterly, then mend itself.

But of course it had not mended entirely, as my life had also not mended entirely. There was a barrier between us, the thin but indestructible memory of what we had been to each other that winter. I was never sure just how much he knew about the way I'd felt about him then, or even whether my mother had told him my lie about his death, but I knew he was aware that I hadn't been a good son. Perhaps the barrier between us could have been broken with a single word—the word *love* or its synonym *forgive*—but as if by mutual pact we never spoke of that difficult winter or its consequences.

Only once did we come close to discussing it. He and my mother had come to visit me and my family in Minneapolis, and we had just finished our Sunday dinner. Caroline and my mother were clearing the table, Sam was playing on the kitchen floor with the dump truck my parents had bought him for his birthday, and my father and I were sitting in the living room watching "Sixty Minutes." The black pastor of a Pentecostal church in Texas was talking to Morley Safer about "the Spirit that descends upon us and inhabits our hearts." Then the camera cut to a black woman standing in the midst of a clapping congregation, her eyes tightly closed and her face glowing with sweat as she rocked back and forth, speaking the incoherent language of angels or demons. Her syllables rose and fell, then mounted in a syntax of spiraling rapture until finally, overcome by the voice that had spoken through her, she sank to her knees, trembling, her eyes open and glistening. The congregation clapped harder then, some of them leaping and dancing as if their bodies were lifted by the collapse of hers, and they yelled, "Praise God!" and "Praise the Lord God Almighty!"

I glanced at my father, who sat watching this with a blank face, and wondered what he was thinking. Then, when the camera moved to another Pentecostal minister discussing a transcript of the woman's speech, a transcript he claimed contained variations on ancient Hebrew and Aramaic words she couldn't possibly have known, I turned to him and asked, in a hesitant way, whether he wanted to keep watching or change channels.

My father's milky blue eyes looked blurred, as if he were looking at something a long way off, and he cleared his throat before he spoke. "It's up to you," he said. "Do you want to watch it?"

I paused. Then I said, "No" and changed the channel.

Perhaps if I had said yes, we might have talked about that terrible day he put a gun to his head and I could have told him what I had since grown to realize—that I loved him. That I had always loved him, though behind his back, without letting him know it. And, in a way, behind my back, too. But I didn't say yes, and in the seven years that remained of his life, we never came as close to ending the winter that was always, for us, an unspoken but living part of our present.

That night, though, unable to sleep, I got up and went into my son's room. Standing there in the wan glow of his night light, I listened to him breathe for a while, then quietly took down the railing we'd put on his bed to keep him from rolling off and hurting himself. Then I sat on the edge of the bed and began to stroke his soft, reddish blond hair. At first he didn't wake, but his forehead wrinkled and he mumbled a little dream-sound.

I am not a religious man. I believe, as my father must have, the day he asked me to save him, that our children are our only salvation, their love our only redemption. And that night, when my son woke, frightened by the dark figure leaning over him, and started to cry, I picked him up and rocked him in my arms, comforting him as I would after a nightmare. "Don't worry," I told him over and over, until the words sounded as incomprehensible to me as they must have to him, "it's only a dream. Everything's going to be all right. Don't worry."

ADG — 0881

7/16/96
APP

PS
3560
A8
B57
1996